CLANDESTINE BABY

NICOLE HELM

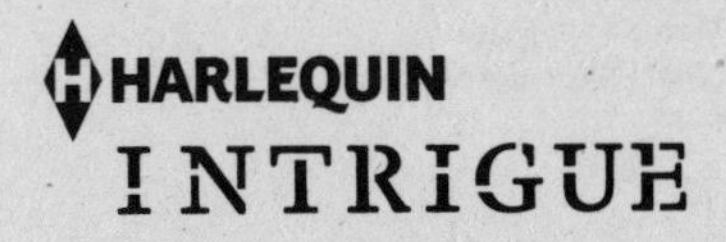

For anyone who's ever found their family outside of the one they were born into.

Recycling programs for this product may not exist in your area.

ISBN-13: 978-1-335-59110-4

Clandestine Baby

For questions and comments about the quality of this book, please contact us at CustomerService@Harlequin.com.

Harlequin Enterprises ULC
22 Adelaide St. West, 41st Floor
Toronto, Ontario M5H 4E3, Canada
www.Harlequin.com

Printed in U.S.A.

Nicole Helm grew up with her nose in a book and the dream of one day becoming a writer. Luckily, after a few failed career choices, she gets to follow that dream—writing down-to-earth contemporary romance and romantic suspense. From farmers to cowboys, Midwest to *the* West, Nicole writes stories about people finding themselves and finding love in the process. She lives in Missouri with her husband and two sons, and dreams of someday owning a barn.

Books by Nicole Helm

Harlequin Intrigue

Covert Cowboy Soldiers

The Lost Hart Triplet
Small Town Vanishing
One Night Standoff
Shot in the Dark
Casing the Copycat
Clandestine Baby

A North Star Novel Series

Summer Stalker
Shot Through the Heart
Mountainside Murder
Cowboy in the Crosshairs
Dodging Bullets in Blue Valley
Undercover Rescue

A Badlands Cops Novel

South Dakota Showdown
Covert Complication
Backcountry Escape
Isolated Threat
Badlands Beware
Close Range Christmas

Visit the Author Profile page at Harlequin.com.

CAST OF CHARACTERS

Cal Thompson—Former soldier turned rancher. Secretly married to Norah Young—but he thought she was dead.

Norah Young—Cal's wife, but she thought he was dead.

Evelyn Marie Young—Cal and Norah's baby daughter.

Jake, Brody, Landon, Henry and Dunne Thompson—Cal's military brothers, now acting as ranching brothers.

Zara and Hazeleigh Hart—Original owners of the ranch, live on the property, seeing Jake and Landon respectively.

Jessie and Quinn Peterson—Twin sisters, live on the property, seeing Henry and Dunne respectively.

Sarabeth Peterson—Jessie's twelve-year-old daughter.

Kate Phillips—Brody's fiancée, lives on the property.

Hero—Norah's giant mutt.

Chapter One

The dog wouldn't stop barking.

Cal Thompson frowned, walking closer and closer to the incessant yelps. Considering he didn't *have* a dog, his best guess was that a stray had maybe been hit on the old country road on the ranch border and no one had stopped to help the poor creature out.

Now it would be his problem. A common occurrence in his life. Cal Young's entire life had been cleaning up other people's messes…before he'd been declared dead, had left the military and moved to this out-of-the-way ranch in the middle of nowhere, Wyoming.

This version of himself, Cal *Thompson*, was supposed to be your everyday rancher, running the old Hart place with his brothers.

The men he ran the ranch with *were* his brothers, if not biologically. They'd fought together for years, had been a team that had taken down terrorist organizations all over the Middle East. Until a clerical error of all things had made their identities known, and they'd needed to be erased.

In Cal's estimation, not much had changed. Sure, he was a rancher now, and he had a different last name, but he still cleaned up problems. They just didn't tend to be in war zones. He still considered himself a sort of de facto leader of their group—which now wasn't just his five brothers, but their various significant others, and one twelve-year-old belonging to one such significant other.

Every group/family/whatever needed a leader, and everyone tended to look to him to be it. Habit or because he was just good at it? It didn't matter. When shots needed to be called, he was usually the one calling them.

He preferred it that way.

Cal finally saw the dog. It was over the fence and in the ditch next to the highway. But it appeared to be fine as it ran toward him, then back to the ditch, over and over, as if trying to signal Cal to come closer.

Cal got the very distinct feeling he wouldn't like what the dog wanted him to see. And while he always listened to his gut, he rarely worried about what he *wanted.* He tended to focus on what needed to be done.

So he moved forward and hopped the fence, watching the big, hairy beast warily. He liked dogs well enough, but there was no telling what kind of stray this was—especially when he was practically the size of one of their horses.

But then he forgot all about the dog, because the dog was leading him to a body.

Cal hurried forward. A woman's body was lying in the ditch, motionless. Dark hair matted with dirt and, potentially, blood draped around some kind of bundle. There was a slight rise and fall of the chest, so the woman wasn't dead.

He supposed that was something.

The dog pranced around the woman, still barking. But it didn't growl as Cal moved closer and carefully crouched next to the woman.

"Good dog," he murmured, then very carefully rolled the woman over. Her head lolled, she didn't open her eyes, but none of that mattered.

Everything stopped. The barking. The wind. His heart.

It couldn't be.

And then the little bundle the woman's body had been shielding began to wriggle. Then wail. The dog whimpered. The breeze picked up again, and Cal's long forgotten heart began to thud against his chest once again.

It was a baby.

My baby?

He pushed that thought away, because it didn't matter. Nothing mattered. Except getting them safe. And to do that he had to somehow shove all of the emotions whirling around in his head away—far away.

He pulled his cell out of his pocket and called Henry, who he knew was out in the truck. He ignored the fact that his hands shook. "Henry, I need the truck about a mile west of the east entrance. Near the ditch of the highway." Was that his voice? Tinny and weak?

"What's up?"

"I found someone in the ditch. She's hurt. I need your help. Get Dunne if he's close. Hurry." He pressed End on the call. He shoved his phone back into his pocket and then, struggling to keep his arms from shaking, reached out and picked up the crying baby.

The bundle was still warm, whether because they hadn't been here long or because… He looked at the woman.

Norah.

Maybe it was some kind of…twin situation. Like Jessie and Quinn, who'd grown up not knowing about each other despite being identical twins. Maybe…

But he knew… He knew it was Norah, and this baby…

He looked down as the baby wailed. "Shh," he murmured, holding the child close to his chest. He reached out and put his fingers at Norah's pulse. Steady, but she was completely unconscious. There was a bloody gash on her forehead, which didn't look as new as he might have liked. How long had she been out here? Bleeding and unconscious?

He looked at the dog and tried to make sense of any of this, but there was no sense to be had.

Norah was supposed to be dead. Not a mother. Not here.

There were so many emotions battering him—

hope, fear, confusion and the desperate desire to understand how—that the time actually passed quickly and Henry's truck appeared on the rise.

Reluctantly, Cal stood to wave him down, baby in his arms. The child had quieted a little, but still made odd noises that made Cal's stomach feel like leaden knots.

Henry parked and both he and Dunne hopped out.

Henry swore, Dunne said nothing. Par for the course. "Someone dump a…"

Then they both looked down at Cal's feet. Dunne immediately went into combat medic mode to assess the situation, but he paused for a moment to look up at Cal. Eyes mirroring all the shock that had slammed into Cal.

"But…"

Cal shook his head. "I don't know."

Henry swore again. "Get her in the truck?"

Dunne nodded. They worked together to pick up Norah's limp body and move her.

"It'll be too much jostling to try to get her inside. Let's lay her out in the back. Cal?"

Cal was already moving to grab a blanket out of the back of the truck. He spread it out in the bed, doing his best work one handed, with a baby cradled in the other arm.

Dunne and Henry worked in silence to place Norah carefully in the bed of the truck.

"Should we take her to the hospital?" Henry asked as Dunne crouched over her, taking her pulse, examining her the same way he'd examine any fallen soldier in a war zone.

"Someone tried to kill her," Cal said. He didn't know that for sure, but based on everything he'd seen, what other conclusion could he draw? There'd been blood. A struggle. Maybe not in that ditch, but somewhere.

Dunne looked over at him, knowing what that meant—keep her away from places she could be traced. "I can take care of the wounds at the ranch, but the lack of consciousness worries me, and I don't know a damn thing about babies, Cal."

"Jessie does."

Dunne sighed, but then nodded. "Quickly."

Henry hurried to the driver's seat. Cal didn't have to whistle for the dog. It seemed intent on following the woman and the baby, and hopped right in behind them.

Dunne kept Norah stable, and Cal sat in the bed of the truck, a whimpering baby in his arms and a similarly whimpering dog snuggling up next to him as Henry drove them back to the ranch house.

Norah made a noise. She didn't move. It was just a kind of groan. Dunne kept his hand on her shoulder, but looked up at Cal. "I guess it might not be her. We've got identical triplets and twins running around. It could be…"

But Cal shook his head. He wished he could believe it. A twin would make more sense, but he knew. "It's Norah." He stared down at the little baby in his arms.

A girl, if the pink blanket and hat were anything to go by. *Mine?* he wondered again.

He didn't know.

"She's supposed to be dead," Cal said, not sure what else to say. Not sure…of anything in the moment.

"Yeah," Dunne agreed. "But so are we."

SHE AWOKE FROM the pain of black and fear to…peace. Warmth. Something smelled vaguely familiar but she couldn't place it. She blinked her eyes open, and the pain started creeping in. Everything hurt—her body, breathing, opening her eyes. Screaming agony everywhere, but she knew she needed to wake up because…

The baby. She had to… She had to protect the baby. She managed to look around. She was lying in a bed in a spacious room. Sunlight streamed through the windows. It was spartan, but not…scary.

Still, she didn't recognize anything. She couldn't… "My baby." Her throat hurt, and her words were garbled. She couldn't remember anything… anything…except her baby. Safe. Her baby…

Why couldn't she think of a name? Her baby's name? Her name? Anything that had happened?

A woman appeared in her vision, a little bundle tucked into her arm. The baby. *Her* baby. She tried to reach out, but couldn't get her arms to move enough. Everything hurt and she had to close her eyes again.

"Your baby is just fine," the woman said. "Why

don't I hold on to her until you're feeling a little stronger?"

Stronger. She definitely didn't feel strong. She wasn't sure what she felt. She tried to open her eyes again. She had to figure something out.

"Where am..." Her gaze tracked the room and stopped on a man who stood at the doorway, and she felt...something. He looked grim and forbidding, but his eyes were... Were they familiar? Did she know him?

She thought she should know him. She thought... She couldn't come up with anything. Anything besides keeping the baby safe.

Was he the man who'd done this to her? Should she...

"Norah," he said, and his voice was dark and low and she thought dimly she should be scared, but she was desperate for him to say more.

She thought that must be the name of the woman holding the baby, but he was looking at her. Was that her name?

She couldn't remember.

"I don't understand." Anything. *Anything.*

The woman sat in a chair next to the bed, giving her a good view of the baby. "I'm Jessie," she said, calmly and soothingly. "What's your little one's name?"

She looked into the baby's blue eyes, and the baby smiled at her. Her heart filled with a joy she didn't understand. But no name came to mind. "I don't know," she whispered.

The Jessie woman flicked a glance to the man at the door. He nodded and disappeared.

"I don't know anything. Her name. My name." Tears began to fill her eyes. She didn't know…

"You've been hurt," Jessie said, laying a hand on her cheek. It didn't soothe out all the panic, but it settled her some. A warm, calm anchor.

"Very hurt," the woman continued. "But you're safe now. I can promise you that."

She swallowed. The pain was a raw, throbbing thing, but she had to speak. "That man… He called me Norah."

Jessie looked at the empty doorway, some indecision on her face. "He did. He thinks you're a woman he used to know."

"Used to?"

The woman shifted in the chair to give her a better look at the baby. "Why don't we call you Norah for now? What would you like us to call the baby? It doesn't have to be right."

Norah looked at the baby—hers, somehow she knew the girl was hers—but no names, nicknames or otherwise would form in her head.

"I don't know. I just don't know." And then she began to cry.

Chapter Two

Cal had talked to a doctor whom Dunne had found through an old military contact they could trust to keep things confidential, and she was coming to the house later today with some equipment that could do the necessary scans. She'd check out the baby too, though there seemed to be no outward trauma there.

Norah didn't remember, and Cal didn't know what to feel. It was both a blessing and a curse. There was so much…emotion mixed up in remembering. But without her memory, it was hard to determine who was after her.

And why her father had lied to him about her untimely death last year.

He looked around at his brothers. They were situated in the living room, Landon at his computer, but the rest of them staring at Cal. Waiting on an explanation.

They knew some things, but not much. Certainly not that he and Norah had gotten secretly married before he'd shipped out with them on their last mission as Team Breaker. He'd never even fully admitted he'd had a relationship with Norah. She'd been their superior officer's daughter after all.

"I can't come up with any death records on her," Landon said, squinting at his computer screen.

"Her father told me she was dead." Cal knew it didn't matter what he told his brothers now. Eventually he'd have to tell them everything if that baby was his and...how could it not be? Jessie said she figured the baby was around four or five months old. The timing was *him*.

And still he said nothing about that to his brothers, to the closest thing he had to a family.

"There's absolutely no record of that being so. In fact, I can find records of her continuing to live a fairly normal life for the past year and a half. Bills and taxes paid. Doctor exams, hospital records for the baby being born. Well, this is something. I found the birth certificate, so we can get the baby's name."

Landon typed away and Cal stood there...saying nothing. He should say something. He should explain, but he couldn't get his body to do what he wanted. He felt frozen. Wound so tight it was a wonder he didn't shatter apart.

It was all too much and...

Landon looked up at him over the computer screen. "Cal."

He saw it in Landon's eyes, and still he couldn't... "What?"

The silence stretched out as Landon studied him.

"So, you're reasonably aware of what's on that child's birth certificate?"

All his brother's gazes seemed to intensify on him. He found he had to clear his throat. "I didn't know, but you add it up, I figured…"

"You figured *what*?" Henry demanded.

When Cal said nothing, because his throat was too tight and because he still hadn't fully accepted or dealt with this himself, Landon shook his head.

"The kid is *his*." Landon looked back down at his screen. "Evelyn Marie Young. What the *hell*, Cal? This says Norah's last name is Young, too, and that you're married? Norah didn't seem like the type to lie or forge records."

Evelyn Marie. His mother's name and her mother's name. His real last name.

And yet, Norah had never had any contact with him after her father had told him she was dead. She hadn't called or written, and he hadn't been declared dead until the end of his mission, when there'd been a mistake…

He'd always taken all that at surface value, but now there were questions. Now he *wondered*.

"Cal."

Cal managed to look up at Brody, who was staring at him with that calm, direct way he had. They all wanted answers, and likely deserved them, but Cal still wanted to keep them wrapped up in all the ice he'd used to just…get through the day without mourning.

And now there wasn't anything to mourn because Norah was *here*, and he had a daughter. *Evelyn Marie.*

"We got married about a week before we shipped out." The words basically fell out of his mouth. Little bombs he didn't know how to disarm or detonate. So they just sat there, between them. Explosions punctuating all that quiet.

"And kept it a secret?" Jake asked, carefully. Oh so carefully. "From us?"

Cal felt wrapped up in a thick fog, so many competing emotions they just sat on his shoulders like a weight. "She didn't think her father would approve. Or I didn't. I don't know. I look back and it's…a blur." Which wasn't exactly a lie because he'd tried so hard to forget.

In a way, it made her amnesia almost ironic. He'd been told she was dead. Car accident. Head-on collision. The woman he'd loved, dead, while he was in the Middle East trying to infiltrate terrorist groups.

So he'd done everything to forget she'd ever existed. To get through the day, the mission. He hadn't cared then so much if he died, but he'd had brothers to keep safe and so he had.

And just like then, these were his brothers. His only family left, or so he'd thought. He owed them more than *I don't remember.*

"We just… We both wanted to keep it a secret until I could be done with the military. So her father couldn't… She wasn't afraid of him—she was afraid of what he'd do to my position. And I was afraid of how it would affect you all and our mission. So we didn't tell anyone. No one. She was going to get things settled while I was deployed. Ready for when we came back and then I'd retire from the military. Do something—anything—else, so we could tell everyone. So we could..." *Start a family.*

He sucked in a breath. There was a sharp, stabbing pain that caught in his chest. It threatened to take him out at the knees. "I didn't know about the baby. We'd only been gone a week when her father called and told me she was dead."

And that was the point. The jumble of things that didn't make sense started from that moment. "The point is, her father told me she was dead. And for the past year plus, she hasn't been. But someone *recently* tried to kill her. I may not be a doctor, but I know those injuries weren't accidents. And she's *here*, and that can't be one either. It has to connect, and we need to get to the bottom of it before someone tries to finish the job. She doesn't remember, so we have to figure it out."

"We will," Jake said calmly, but he looked down at his own wedding ring, twisted it around his finger. "But this is about more than figuring out danger, Cal. You're a husband and a father."

"And you didn't tell us," Henry added, his arms crossed over his chest. "All this time. Even when we found out she'd died, you didn't tell us you'd been *married.*"

"I wasn't going to compromise the mission." That had been the thing he'd held on to. He'd needed that. Something to focus on that wasn't the excruciating pain of losing the woman who'd…found a way under all his scars. Turned him inside out and somehow made him whole.

It was better to be pieces. Compartments. Easier. Stronger.

Henry muttered an oath. Landon made a snort of disgust. The rest of them rolled their eyes.

"We're done with missions," Brody said firmly.

"I'm not," Cal said distinctly, because how else was he going to get through this? "*This* is my mission. Someone wanted me to think she was dead, and now someone's trying to make that a reality. I won't let that happen."

"We won't," Brody agreed. "But if you don't take some time to deal with the fact your secret wife is *alive,* and you have a child…that mission is going to break you. So take a minute. Deal."

Deal. *Deal?* How was he ever supposed to deal with this lost year? With being a father to a baby who…

A knock on the door sounded and Dunne stood. "That should be the doctor."

Cal nodded, glad for the interruption. Because nothing about what he felt or was dealing with was important. Norah and Evelyn being okay and safe was what was important.

The end.

NORAH LAY IN bed while the doctor hooked up machines and asked her questions.

She was trying to think of herself as Norah, so when someone addressed her with that name she responded. She couldn't say it felt right, but what did?

She looked down at the baby dozing in her arms. Well, this did.

Norah was strong enough to hold the baby now while the doctor went through tests, and more questions. So many questions she didn't have any answers for. She didn't remember anything.

When the doctor was finished, she took a seat in the chair next to the bed. Like all the women who'd come in to help, she had a kind smile and a reassuring demeanor.

"For everything you've been through, you're in decent shape. You've had a nasty concussion, quite a few bumps, bruises, lacerations." There was a slight hesitation, then the doctor reached out and gently touched her neck. "Someone tried to strangle you."

She—*Norah*—reached up to touch her neck with her free hand. *Strangle*. "That's..."

"Scary, I know. And it explains why you're struggling to remember. Your body experienced trauma—physically and emotionally—and your brain is working hard to deal with that. While it does, it's either forgetting or blocking out information in your memory." The doctor smiled kindly. "I believe that as your body heals, your brain will too. There's no physical damage that caused the memory loss that

I see. I'll get a few consults on the tests I ran, but whether you remember everything or not, you are going to be okay."

Norah nodded, even though her heart beat double time in her chest. Someone had tried to *strangle* her? Left her for dead in a ditch or…

"As for this sweetheart," the doctor said, stroking the baby's cheek, "she's in great shape. No signs of injury or malnutrition or anything that indicates she'd been left uncared for for long. Whatever happened, you protected your little girl."

Norah looked down at the baby. Whose name she also didn't know. "You really think… I'll remember?"

"I do. But be patient with yourself. Your body needs to heal. You need to rest. Once all that happens, the likelihood of your memory returning gets higher and higher."

"Thank you."

"I'll likely want to do a checkup in a few weeks, or if you have any symptoms crop up—headache, nausea, insomnia…anything out of the ordinary, you'll get in contact with me ASAP, okay?"

"I don't know what the ordinary is," Norah replied. The doctor's diagnosis didn't settle her any. If anything, she felt more adrift. There were no answers. Only time and rest.

"You've got quite the crew here taking care of you and your baby. It's going to be all right."

The door behind the doctor opened and one of

the men stood there. Cal, she thought. He seemed to come more than anyone else aside from Jessie, who was almost always around to help with the baby.

This man never smiled. He rarely spoke. But he was so often *here*. Looking at her with the same dark, unreadable gaze.

"I'm going to consult with an expert on brain injuries, make sure I'm not far off," the doctor said. She looked at the man in the doorway. "Don't worry. It'll all be done anonymously, and I'll get back to you as soon as I can."

He nodded and said nothing, just ushered the doctor out of the room. Norah was surprised that he returned, and even came to sit down on the chair next to her bed.

She didn't know what to say to him. Clearly he knew her. He was the one who'd said her name. Every time he was in here, he looked at her...with some kind of expectation in his eyes he tried to hide. But she saw it.

"How are you doing?" he asked.

Norah took a deep breath and studied him—rather than try to remember who he was, she simply collected facts. He was objectively handsome, if a little severe. His eyes were dark, his jaw sharp. He was tall and broad and she thought maybe she should be afraid. He had big hands, certainly capable of strangling her.

But even as she searched his face, his eyes, and

saw nothing but a grim kind of disconnect, she didn't feel scared of him.

"I just wish I remembered."

The man—Cal—nodded. She knew he was… something to her. Just in the way he acted around her. Jessie was kind and warm but didn't act like she knew her. The other men who came in and out were the same. But this man, he had pain in his eyes and she felt a soul-deep yearning to ease it.

"I think the important thing is to rest. Heal." He stared at the baby with an intensity Norah couldn't understand. And it gave her the courage to finally ask…

"How do we know each other?"

His dark eyes rose to meet hers, but he didn't hold her gaze. He looked back down. "Well…"

"Please, just tell me the truth. The doctor said someone tried to strangle me. I don't remember *anything*."

"You need to rest and—"

"I need to understand *something*," she insisted, trying not to cry. It felt imperative to just…be strong somehow. Deal with this somehow. But she had to know something—she had to have some fact to hold on to.

"We found the birth certificate for the baby. Her name is Evelyn."

Norah looked down at the baby, whose blue eyes were the same as what she'd seen in the mirror when

Jessie had helped her clean up a little bit. But Norah had blond hair and the baby's hair was dark.

Like this man.

But if he didn't know the baby's name until he'd found the birth certificate… "You knew me before I had a baby? But not after?"

He looked up at her again. "Yes."

"Yes. Yes…? That's it? Just yes?" She knew she shouldn't start panicking, but she couldn't seem to help it. She tried to shift without waking the baby, without making her body throb with all the aches and pains the painkillers only moderately dulled. "I'm lying in this house I don't know with a baby I don't know. Random people walk in and out. That doctor… Maybe she wasn't a doctor." Her voice was getting more and more shrill with every word, but she'd held herself under control for so long and he…they all just patted her on the head and said it would be fine.

It wasn't fine. "I don't know anything! I don't know—"

The baby—Evelyn—scrunched up her face, and whimpers quickly turned to wails of distress.

"I'm sorry, baby. I'm so sorry." She rocked the baby, and the tears began to fall. She figured she had a good reason to cry, and still there was embarrassment with the tears. "How do I even know she's mine? How do I even know I'm safe? You could have strangled me. You could be the bad guy."

"She's yours." His jaw tensed, but he held her gaze

for once. "I don't want to hurt you, Norah. I've never wanted to hurt you."

"Not knowing hurts me." She sniffled, but she held the baby to her chest rather than wipe away the tears. It was a bit like a pressure valve. A few tears and she felt less like exploding. More capable of taking this step-by-step.

But she needed somewhere to take that step from. "How do you know me?" she repeated.

He hesitated again, looked down at his big hands. She could tell, somehow, that he was deciding what to say. But it was better than nothing.

"We met a few years ago. I was in the military and your father was my superior officer."

Father. Military? None of it rang any bells.

"We..." He trailed off and his eyebrows drew together. Usually she couldn't read his expression beyond intensity, but she saw uncertainty there now.

"Just say it. *Say* it. How am I supposed to rest and relax when everyone around me knows more about me than I do?"

"We hit it off," he said, as if each word was some great admission. "You didn't think your father would approve, and I was in no rush to upset my superior officer—a man I looked up to. The first time I deployed, we both kind of accepted that was it."

She tried to imagine *hitting it* off with this man, but he was so serious. So aloof and cold. Of course, she couldn't even remember herself. Maybe she was serious too.

When he gave nothing else, she pressed. "But it wasn't it?" She kept…studying him. Trying to find truth in any of these words. This was clearly no happy, tearful reunion. He was so tense. So brittle. Every word was an admission he didn't want to make.

Somehow that made it seem like the truth.

"No, I came back. We ran into each other. Nothing…" He was staring at his hands, shaking his head. "Nothing had changed. We…were in love with each other."

She tried to imagine *loving* this man, loving anyone. But it all felt like a blank—not just the truth, but any feelings about the truth she was supposed to have.

"I still had some time left, a secret mission your father wanted me to lead up. It required another deployment, a particularly dangerous one. But… I don't know, I guess we were both foolish enough to think it didn't matter. A week before I shipped out, we got married. Secretly."

He took a deep breath and before she could even try to wrap her head around being *married* to him, he pressed on. The information seeming to pour out of him now. "Not a week later, I was informed you'd died. I never heard from you again and had no reason to doubt it. Then I found you in a ditch near my property. With this baby. And that giant dog. Far away from *everything* that was our life together. So, I don't have the answers we need, Norah. I only *know* the bare minimum more than you do."

She'd asked for one thing, and he'd certainly given it to her. "We're…married."

"I don't even know what we are. I was told you were dead. I don't know what you were told."

"The baby…"

"My name is on the birth certificate, but I wasn't… I don't know."

He seemed like the kind of man who desperately struggled with the phrase *I don't know*, which almost seemed humorous considering she was currently in a constant state of not knowing. Down to… "Am I the kind of person who'd have an affair? Because if not, this baby has to be yours, doesn't it?"

Cal shook his head. "Like I said, I don't know what you were told. You might not have thought we were married. You might have been told I was dead, too. But the timing…" He cleared his throat. He seemed to wrap himself in something…cold. Detached. What little break in all of that was gone. "It's likely she's mine," he said flatly.

Norah looked down at the baby, who'd snuggled into her chest. There was a comfort in holding the warm body against her, feeling the rise and fall of her breathing. She was beautiful, and even when Norah hadn't known anything, she'd known her only job was to protect this little one.

"I don't remember… None of this sounds familiar, but nothing does. I don't know who'd want to strangle me. I don't understand any of this, but I know when I woke up…the only thing I remembered was that I had to keep her safe."

"I'm sure you're a wonderful mother," Cal said, but he was still distant, and he stood carefully. "I'll go get Jessie to come take her so you can get some rest. The doctor insisted that rest is imperative."

Norah looked from the baby to him. He was already backing toward the door, but no. Not after all that.

"If she's yours, shouldn't you take her?"

Chapter Three

Cal stood frozen. *Shouldn't you take her?* No doubt. But he knew nothing about babies. He was already too…ripped apart. He hadn't meant to tell Norah *everything*, but it had poured out of him. A dam break of words.

Now, he needed to find a way to build that dam back up. Take control of the situation.

And she wanted him to take this baby. This child.

Evelyn Marie. Yours.

All the while Norah's blue eyes studied him, still looking for the answers. Answers he didn't have.

But would.

Stiffly he moved back toward the bed. The baby was curled up on Norah's chest. He didn't have the first clue how to lift a baby. How to do anything with her.

If she's yours, shouldn't you take her?

He didn't have the first clue how to be a father. He'd never known his own. He and Norah had spoken of building a family as a fuzzy future. Not a real, living breathing certainty.

But how could he admit to Norah he didn't know what to do with a baby when she couldn't remember *anything*? He had to be the one in control. The one who handled things. She'd been hurt and she couldn't remember.

So, he had to step up.

Stiffly, he bent over the bed and managed to shift the baby into his arms. The baby let out an odd noise—a mix of displeasure and acceptance. Every time he picked her up—and he did everything in his power to do it as little as possible—he felt like the weight of the world was on his shoulders. He looked down at her now. Small, eyes open, staring up at him like she understood everything even though she was just a baby.

"There's something about her… She does look like you," Norah said softly.

He didn't see it. Or didn't let himself see it. But that ocean of blue… "She has your eyes," he managed, though the words felt choked in his throat.

Norah nodded. He looked at her then. Bruised but patched up. Pale with bags under her eyes. She'd been alive all this time. Then someone had tried to kill her.

"You need your rest," he said, because if he stood here for much longer, cataloging all the ways she was the same and different, he might lose it altogether.

She nodded again, her eyes drooping. "I guess so."

Cal didn't know what else to say. Didn't think he could get the words out even if he did. So, he left her to go back to sleep. He tried to get the dog to come with him, but it refused to leave her bedside unless Sarabeth urged him outside with a treat and to do his business.

Jessie's daughter who now lived with them had that kind of pull with all the animals around the ranch.

Cal tried not to think about how much he owed that dog.

The doctor had eased some of his concerns about Norah and Evelyn's well-being. He was grateful for Jessie's experience as a mother, because she'd immediately made a feeding, changing and sleeping schedule for the child and they all took turns helping take care of her.

Cal stepped into the kitchen, where Sarabeth was sitting at the table, kicking her heels against the legs of the chair. When she saw him, she jumped to her feet. "Can I hold her? I'll be so careful. The careful-est."

Cal looked around, desperate for an adult who knew what they were doing to swoop in and save him, but there was only Sarabeth's insistence and his own confusion.

"I guess," Cal muttered. But everything in the kitchen was hard surfaces and sharp edges. "In the living room. On the couch."

Sarabeth practically danced the whole way there, then settled herself on the couch and held out her arms. Cal carefully transferred the baby, hands clammy, heart beating a little too hard. How did people just…go about their business holding a squirming life?

The baby squealed and grabbed at Sarabeth's braid.

"What's her name?" Sarabeth asked, offering her finger instead of the braid. The girl's chubby fingers closed over Sarabeth's slender ones.

"Evelyn," he said, sounding strangled even to his own ears.

Sarabeth seemed to mull that over as she gazed down at the baby. "That's pretty. Just like you." She stroked the girl's cheek.

It was my mother's name. But he didn't say that to the twelve-year-old currently loving on…not the baby, *his* baby. *His* daughter.

Evelyn. His daughter.

The front door opened and Jessie stepped inside, carrying a few bags. "Oh, good, you've got the baby." Henry followed, looking a bit shell-shocked as he held even more bags. "I picked up a few things for her."

"A few things," Henry muttered. "I think she bought out the store."

Jessie gave him a disapproving look. "We had *nothing* for a baby, honestly, and I think she can roll over both ways. It won't be long before she's crawling. We've got to babyproof. Feed her properly. Dress her. Diapers. Et cetera. And I got a few things for the dog. He shouldn't only be eating scraps."

"Thank you," Cal said stiffly.

Jessie settled in next to Sarabeth, already murmuring sweet things at Evelyn. Sarabeth looked up at her mother.

"Can't you guys have one so I can be a big sister?"

Jessie turned the shade of a tomato but looked up at Henry with a little smile that had Cal looking at Henry too.

"Working on it," Henry muttered with a shrug. Jessie and Sarabeth settled Evelyn onto the ground and held a toy over her, causing her to babble and wriggle in happiness.

"How are you *working on it*?" Cal replied, not sure why that was…surprising.

Henry shrugged and gave Cal a nudge out of the room and into the kitchen. "Bought a ring anyway. We're going to talk the whole marriage thing over with Sarabeth, and adoption and all that jazz, but since she's subtle as a Mack truck, I figure she'll go for it."

"Yeah."

"You can stand there and act surprised, but here we all thought you were the last holdout. Instead, you beat us all to it."

"I don't know how to…" Cal had never been sure he'd know how to be a husband, but he'd trusted Norah to guide him. In that. In building a family, whatever that looked like. But he'd had no real time to worry about it. He'd shipped out and she'd been gone. Dead.

Except she wasn't, and that was the only thought

he could hold in his head at the moment. “I need to go talk to Landon and see what he’s found out about Colonel Elliot.”

“We’ll keep an eye on Evelyn.”

Evelyn. His daughter. Maybe he should be taking care of her, but the only way he really knew how was to figure out who’d tried to kill her mother. And why he’d been told Norah was dead over a year ago. “Thanks.”

He started moving for the back door. Landon was living with Hazeleigh in her little cabin across the way. He’d either be there or out working on the ranch.

“Listen, Cal…” Henry said, before Cal could go fully out the door. “There’s no handbook for this. No mission plan. It’s life. Not war.”

But it felt a hell of a lot like a war inside of him, and war Cal knew what to do with.

A lot more than he knew what to do with life.

A COUPLE DAYS LATER, Norah was feeling strong enough to move around. Someone had to be with her as she still got a little lightheaded if she got tired, and she didn’t dare hold Evelyn unless she was settled into bed or a chair, but she could tell her health was improving.

Her memory remained a frustrating blank, as blank as the expression forever on Cal’s face as he worked to keep his distance from her and the baby. Though she’d catch him watching her intently from across the room.

Still, if she could set aside her memory loss, there was a certain coziness about the days. One of the women of the ranch was always around to help with Evelyn—mostly Jessie or Sarabeth or Kate. The men were kind, but careful. They tended to stop talking when she entered a room, looking at each other as if they weren't quite sure what to say.

That Norah didn't care for.

On this evening, she'd come into the kitchen to get a little after-dinner snack, the dog trailing behind her. Sarabeth had taken to calling him Brownie, though Norah knew he needed a more admirable name. He was her hero. He'd alerted someone she and Evelyn were there.

"Maybe we'll call you Hero," she said, patting the dog's head as they left her room.

She was hungry and she wanted something sweet and full of calories. Maybe some ice cream. Evelyn was asleep, and Norah was hoping to run into Cal and maybe grill him for more details on all she didn't remember.

He was her husband. Maybe. Sort of. He seemed to dance around the subject with the ease of… Well, she didn't know.

When she walked into the kitchen, all six brothers were there. They went immediately silent.

Norah frowned. "I just came to get a snack."

Cal moved out of the kitchen area and over to the table, giving her ample room to get what she wanted. The dog followed her like a shadow.

She decided to take her sweet time. Scooping ice cream. Adding some chocolate syrup. Whipped cream. Once she'd made herself a rather impressive sundae, she went straight to the table, took an open seat and settled herself down to eat.

And talk. "I think it's time we discussed who tried to kill me," she announced. Hero curled up at her feet.

All six men exchanged glances—and boy, was that annoying.

"Do you remember something?" Cal asked, studying her as if one look and he'd *know* what she remembered.

"No." She'd had a dream last night, something terrifying, but it was misty and confusing in the light of day—and as likely to be fictional as actual memory. "But someone tried to kill me. And you six seem to lurk around talking about it behind my back. I get the impression you're looking into it, and I want to know what you know."

"Don't—"

She pointed her spoon at Cal, fixed him with the sternest look she could manage. "Don't you dare tell me not to worry about it. Someone tried to *kill* me. I want to know what you know."

"It's only fair, Cal," Jake said. She remembered Jake's name because he was the most friendly. He smiled the easiest. And he was married to one of the sets of identical women running about. That *did* make things hard to figure, though Zara and Hazeleigh were so different she could usually distinguish them by clothes.

Jessie and her twin sister, Quinn, were harder, but they spoke a little differently and Quinn had no interest in fussing over the baby like Jessie did.

The men all looked different despite the fact they were brothers, but they acted so much the same she had a hard time remembering name to name. But Jake was speaking, urging Cal to give her some information.

Cal scowled, but when all the other brothers nodded along, he sighed heavily. Then he took a seat across from her.

"We've started from the beginning. When your father told me you were dead. There's no evidence anywhere anyone else thought you were dead." He kept his eyes on her face, like he was constantly looking for signs of distress. "So, I started looking into your father."

"You say that like you're worried about my reaction, but I don't *remember* my father."

"But I do, and you loved him. After your mother died, you took care of him. You were the light of his life."

"Okay. So, you think he found out about us? Tried to kill me?"

"Strangulation is a personal attack, typically. But he told me you were dead one week into my mission. The attack on you didn't happen until recently—which is over a year later. They might be related, but the time between suggests not so directly."

Norah rubbed her temple. Everything was starting to throb. "Does he always talk in circles like this?" she muttered to the men sitting around the table.

"Yes," they all replied emphatically, causing Cal to frown deeply.

"I have the skills to get any information that might be out there," one of the brothers said. The one that lived with Hazeleigh in the cabin across the yard. Landon. "I was able to find Evelyn's birth certificate, your bill payment history for the past year, but there's nothing about you actually being dead. So, I started digging into Colonel Elliot—your father. I didn't get far when I found a police report. You reported your father missing three weeks ago."

Norah didn't feel anything, because whether Colonel Elliot was her father or not, it was all a blank. She didn't *remember* him. She couldn't think of what he looked like or what he'd done for her.

Still, Cal had said she'd been the light of her father's life. "So, he went missing three weeks ago, and a few days ago someone tried to kill me. Is it connected? Or is he the attacker?"

If Cal was surprised by her lack of emotional connection, neither he nor his brothers showed it. "We don't know," Cal said grimly. "But we're going to find out."

Chapter Four

Eventually, Cal convinced Norah to go back to sleep with not much more information than that. Not that he had all that many more details, but he had the beginnings of a plan. By the morning, he had a fully formed one, if next to no sleep in the meantime.

Still, he went to do his morning ranch chores, and explained everything to his brothers.

"I should go to DC."

Cal knew the plan wouldn't go over well with anyone. He'd thought about just leaving—sneaking out in the dead of night, not giving them a chance to talk him out of it, but it was better if they worked together. They'd find answers sooner, and Norah and the baby might be safe here, but Cal still knew the sooner they had answers the better.

Maybe he'd be able to really breathe with a few answers.

"Sorry. Not happening," Brody replied, saddling one of the horses. As if *he* were in charge.

Cal opened his mouth to argue, to issue an *order*, but Henry shook his head from his spot pitching hay.

"We discussed it before you got out here. Sure, we need to do some groundwork in DC, get to the bottom of Elliot's disappearance, but it's not going to be you."

"Oh, really?" Cal replied coolly. "Because it's your wife and child on the line?"

"The wife and child you're avoiding like the plague?" Jake offered, just as coolly, which wasn't like him at all.

Cal scowled.

"We went through all the options," Henry said. "Including you, but you should be here with them. In case Norah remembers something. In case she takes a turn for the worse. She's—they're both—your responsibility. So, you stay put. Dunne will stay in case Norah or the baby need medical attention. Jake runs enough of the day-to-day at the ranch with Zara, it's not a great time for him to take off. Jessie's instrumental in taking care of Evelyn, so I'll stay put with her and Sarabeth. We were going to go with Brody, but apparently *everyone's* got secrets."

Cal turned to Brody, who had his hands shoved in his pockets. He rocked back on his heels. "Not a secret," Brody replied, and it was strange to watch him try to fight back a smile as he explained why he'd be staying put. "Kate was wanting to keep it on the down low a few more weeks, but she's pregnant.

She doesn't really feel up to traveling, and we think going in couples would be good for optics."

Marriages. Babies. Things his brothers had chosen in this new life of theirs. Brody smiling. It caught him off guard enough that he couldn't mount an argument.

Henry continued the plan they'd formed without consulting him. "That leaves Landon."

"I'll take Hazeleigh," Landon said. "We'll tour the museums by day, lay a nice cover, then I'll do some investigating by night. I'm the least likely to be recognized, and it'll just look like a vacation to anyone who might be paying attention."

"You're going to take Hazeleigh straight into danger like that?" Cal demanded.

"Staying put is danger too," Landon replied with a shrug. "If someone tried to kill Norah, and they realize they failed, don't you think they'll come to finish the job? And when they do, don't you think they'll look into who helped her? And if it *does* connect to Colonel Elliot, then the chances of it connecting to us—the *before* us—are pretty high too."

Cal had thought of all that, so he shouldn't be surprised his brothers had as well. "It's an unnecessary risk."

"It isn't," Brody replied. "It's a necessary risk."

Cal could argue. He could demand everyone back off and let him handle it, but things had changed. He was no longer the commanding officer. Even if he was something like *a* leader, his word wasn't law.

Much as he'd like it to be.

Still... "I should be the one to go. I don't have—"

"You have a wife and kid, remember?" Dunne said in his quiet way. "If this does connect to Colonel Elliot—good or bad—we are *all* potentially connected. It's *all* our danger. So, we're all going to get to the bottom of it. Landon and Hazeleigh will leave tomorrow. They'll spend five days tops in DC. If Landon finds info, great. If not, we'll move to plan B."

"And in the interim, we'll make sure no one comes to finish the job on Norah," Jake said, leading his horse toward the stable doors. "I'm late to meet Zara in the east field. I'll be back at lunch."

"We've all got work to do," Brody said, leading his own horse outside. When Cal took a step toward his horse's pen, Henry stopped him.

"Not you, buddy. I don't know much about amnesia, and the doctor said rest will help, but I'm guessing being around a face she might actually remember—and fondly, God knows why—is the next best thing. Stay put and deal with your family."

Everyone scattered to do their work around the ranch. Except Dunne and Cal himself, because he felt rooted to this spot in the stables. *Deal with your family.* He hadn't had one for so long, and the blip with Norah before felt like some other...person. A dream, maybe. Because she'd died, like everyone who loved him always did. Colonel Elliot had been so...

"Avoiding them doesn't do anything except put off the inevitable," Dunne said quietly.

Cal had forgotten he wasn't alone. He blinked once, trying to find that inner core of determination that had gotten him through everything. *Everything.*

Inevitable. Norah and the baby—*his* baby—were indeed inevitable, but he hadn't figured out how to make it…right.

He had to make it right, not worse, and that required a certain amount of space. He knew he couldn't explain that to Dunne.

"Is it secret whispering time?" a female voice asked from outside the stable. Quinn popped her head in. "Do you need a third?"

"Just giving Cal a bit of a pep talk."

Quinn's eyebrows rose as she marched toward them, her limp almost unnoticeable these days. "The dull giving the terminally tight-assed a pep talk?" Quinn clucked her tongue. "Sad state of affairs."

"Dull, huh?"

She flashed Dunne a grin, one that spoke of private things Cal had no doubt she'd start talking about right here in front of him if he didn't escape.

"All right," Cal muttered. "I'm out." Causing both Dunne and Quinn to laugh.

Quinn turned to him. "Hold tight. I'm heading into town with Hazeleigh. Norah said she didn't need anything, but she could use some clothes of her own, so we're going to pick out a few things. Plus get Hazeleigh some stuff for her trip. But I wanted to ask you if you've got any hints about her style, you know?"

At Cal's blank look, Quinn rolled her eyes. "Favorite colors? Does she run cold? Like big neon lions to decorate her clothes? Or did you not know anything about your *wife*?"

Cal scowled. "She likes..." He didn't want to remember what she liked. Who she was. It was too hard. Too painful. Even knowing she was alive and right here, it opened some door to a past self he'd tried to kill off.

But Quinn's usually sharp gaze softened with pity, and Cal...hated it. To get *pity* from someone who'd been through everything Quinn had gone through. No. Absolutely not.

"She likes darker colors. Nothing neon. But not dull. Soft, comfortable. She always looked..." *Perfect.* He curled one hand into a fist, trying to stay somehow in the here and now. Danger. Protection. Not memories. "Put together."

Quinn nodded. "That's good, thanks."

"I thought you hated shopping," Dunne said to her. Clearly helping to change the subject because they both *pitied* him.

Cal wanted to punch something.

"Don't worry, I'll only buy a few lethal weapons, sweetie." She waved and disappeared.

"How do you put up with her?" Cal muttered. Quinn did her level best to be outrageous, antagonistic or just plain shocking...the very opposite of Dunne. They made no sense, and yet.

Dunne laughed, a real one, which had always been rare. "Not really sure *how* we put up with each other, but we do."

Cal didn't have to ask if it made him happy. Dunne might not be a light, demonstrative, smiley type guy like Landon was, but dating the irreverent Quinn, and dealing with his family's past, had loosened something inside of him. He was still decidedly his quiet self, but not so dark and brooding any longer.

"It isn't like you to shirk a responsibility," Dunne said after a few moments of watching Quinn walk away.

The commentary was quite unwelcome.

"I'm hardly shirking."

"You're avoiding them. And I get it, Cal. This isn't just a responsibility. You loved her or you wouldn't have married her. You thought she was dead for over a year. It's emotional upheaval, and well, that isn't a strong suit for any of us."

Cal said nothing because it was all too close to the truth.

"But she needs you. Not to know what to do, not to be perfect and have all the answers. Just to be there."

But who was he if he didn't have all the answers?

NORAH WOKE FEELING much stronger. She'd had dreams last night, but in the warm glow of morning couldn't quite put them together. Were they memories? Fictions her mind was playing tricks on her with?

She sighed and sat up carefully. Her body still ached, particularly her throat, but she wasn't dizzy or light-headed.

She got out of bed and padded over to the door, Hero on her heels. They'd come up with a kind of routine. Though Hero rarely left her side, in the morning she would let him out of the room and someone would let him out of the front or back door so he could do his business.

And no matter that they were in the middle of nowhere Wyoming, he never ran off. He always came back to her.

So, she opened the door and he trotted off. Norah walked over to the portable crib where Evelyn slept. She looked down at her daughter and was bowled over by a tide of love. It was so all-encompassing, so big, it very nearly hurt.

This was her baby. She couldn't remember anything, but she held on to the fact Evelyn was hers.

She heard something, thought it was Hero already back, but when she looked over her shoulder Cal stood there in the doorway, that inscrutable look on his face.

She felt…something for him. It wasn't like that wave of love she felt for her daughter. But it wasn't that blank nothingness when she tried to think of her father—whoever he was. There was just this twisting sensation in her chest she didn't know how to describe.

But sometimes she wanted to reach out and stroke

his cheek and tell him it would be okay, just as she did to Evelyn when she fussed.

She looked back down at the baby. "It's so strange," she said conversationally, though she kept her voice near a whisper so as not to disturb Evelyn. "I love her so much. I don't remember anything. Not you. Not my father. But her?" Norah pressed a hand to her chest. "I'm bowled over by this."

"You protected her."

Norah looked up at him. He still stood by the door. She couldn't understand why he held himself so apart. Part of her was glad for it. What would she do if he wanted to act like they were married when he was a stranger to her? Still, she wished he'd…be more than a strange, quiet ghost. "And now you're protecting us."

His face somehow got *more* blank, and she realized it was the wrong thing to say to him. What would be the right thing? She didn't have a clue.

"I thought of something interesting." She turned from Evelyn, moved closer to Cal. Both because she wanted Evelyn to sleep as long as she would, and because she wondered if he'd back away.

He didn't, but he did look wary. Still, she held out her hands.

Cal looked down at them, but she could tell he didn't see what she saw.

"It's your hands."

She rolled her eyes. "Yes, but look at my ring finger." She wiggled it. "I've been laid up for a few days now, but there's still a tan line where rings would have been. It's my right hand, but if it was a secret marriage..."

Cal nodded. "You wore them on your right hand." Each word sounded like a scrape against the quiet.

She had to curl her hands to keep from reaching out. It seemed like a natural thing, to want to comfort him. But maybe that was who she was. Someone who wanted to comfort anyone hurting—and he was clearly hurting, no matter how many layers of stoicism he hid it under. Did she know that because she knew him, or because it was obvious?

She closed her eyes for a moment. The constant loop of questions was just exhausting, but she didn't know how to shut them off. So she tried to focus on what she was trying to tell Cal.

"But you weren't wearing them when I found you," he pointed out. "You don't have them."

"No, but if there's still a tan line, I was wearing them close enough to now that either *I* only took them off a few days before this happened, or they were taken off me. I think it proves that someone told me you were dead," she said. "Just like someone told you. Because if I thought you'd...just, like, gone off on a mission and never spoken to me, I'd be mad. Not still wearing your rings." She hoped, anyway. She didn't want to be the kind of woman who pined after someone who'd clearly left her behind—even if the leaving had been a lie. "I would have tried to tell you about Evelyn, and if I hadn't been able to reach you, knowing you were alive, I'd be furious. Not still wearing your rings."

"I suppose," he said, but his voice was rusty. Like some great emotion held him hostage there. He looked over at the crib but made no move to go see Evelyn sleeping inside.

"Evelyn was my mother's name," he murmured, almost like he hadn't meant to admit that. Maybe he hadn't.

Norah kept her gaze on Cal's face. So stoic. So *tense.* She wanted to reach out, but she didn't dare. "Did I know her?" she asked gently.

He shook his head. "She died when I was thirteen."

"I'm sorry."

He shrugged. "It was something we had in common. Marie was your mother's name."

Norah rubbed at her chest. It was so strange to know she should feel something, and not. "I don't remember. But…if I named her after your mother when you weren't there, again, I had to think you were dead."

Cal swallowed but nodded. "I suppose you're right, but your father told me you were dead. A week after I deployed, and that was over a year ago. If you reported him missing three weeks ago, if nothing documentation-wise proves you were dead, he's behind some part of this. Looking into it… it might not give you the answers you want."

"But if he's missing, doesn't that mean something

happened to him? Maybe he did something bad, but maybe he's a victim."

"But him missing is recent. Him faking our deaths to each other is over a year old."

Norah sighed. "I wish I could feel something about that, but I don't. I can't feel what I don't remember."

"You will. When your memories return, and they will. And you might feel differently about…everything."

He said *everything*, but she had a feeling he meant she'd feel differently about him, when she didn't know how she felt about him in the moment. "Are you afraid I'll still love you, or afraid that I won't?"

He flinched, and it felt like some kind of win that she could affect him enough to make him do that.

"I'm not afraid of anything. The only thing I'm concerned about is your safety." Which did not answer her question.

"Such a soldier," she said, without fully thinking the words through, or what they meant. It just felt like the right thing to say.

This time he didn't flinch, he flat out paled.

"What?" she asked, taking a slight step back at the way he stared at her. It was…unnerving. More intense than usual.

He shook his head, and though he didn't get any of his color back, he spoke in that clipped, closed-off manner again. "Landon and Hazeleigh are going to go to DC and do some investigating."

She could press the previous question, but she got the feeling it would be like beating her head against a brick wall. So, she focused on what this new development meant. “Investigating my father?”

Cal nodded. “His disappearance, what he might have been doing leading up to it.”

Before Norah could decide how to feel about that, Evelyn began to fuss. Norah crossed the room. “Good morning, baby,” she cooed. She picked Evelyn up since she was feeling sturdy. The baby wriggled and made her hunger known.

“She needs a change and a bottle. I’ll change her if you can go get a bottle ready.”

He hesitated, but then nodded once and left the room. Hero trotted back inside the room, someone having let him in. He circled the room, sniffed at the crib, then settled himself in a shaft of sunlight on the floor.

When Cal returned with the bottle, Norah turned to him. The morning feeding was her favorite time. Just her and Evelyn and she could keep some of her questions at bay and just enjoy the moment. But…

Cal was Evelyn’s father, and as little as Norah understood about what that meant or how to move forward, she knew he needed to start interacting with her. “Why don’t you feed her this morning?”

“I don’t know how.”

“Don’t you think you should learn?”

There was something like anguish in his eyes,

a brief flash of it, then gone. As his posture got straighter, somehow, and his jaw tighter.

"Norah, I need you to understand something. Whatever is going on, whoever is out to hurt you, I will find them. I'll solve this for you. But after that? I'm legally dead. I'm not Cal Young anymore. I'm not your husband. I'm not her father. I'm a completely different man, so terrorists don't come after me or anyone I'm connected to. I may not be able to be a part of either of your lives once we know you're safe."

Something that felt like anger stirred in her, though it wasn't fully formed enough to lean into. If he loved her, remembered her, and had married her, shouldn't he want them?

Maybe he did. She thought it sounded like he was trying to protect her, or her feelings. She'd have to think about it a little more, so for now she just nodded. "Then I guess you should spend as much time with her as you can while you can." And she handed him the bottle.

Chapter Five

Cal fed Evelyn, having no choice once Norah walked out of the room. The little girl in his arms, his responsibility and yet… He was a danger to anyone he loved, or who loved him back. He was a ticking time bomb, and the only reason he had his brothers was that they were too.

And look at the families they're building.

Cal wasn't sure how they could be so…optimistic. Sure, they'd been moved here in an attempt by the military to make up for the mistake that had put their lives in danger. "Killed" off and erased and given a fresh, out-of-the-way spot to live. To be.

But if one mistake could be made, more mistakes could. Cal figured it was only a matter of time…

His life had always been only a matter of time, and whenever he'd let himself be fooled into planning a future, the universe had rid him of his delusions real fast.

So, he didn't see how there could possibly be a

future where he knew his daughter without putting her in danger.

He looked down at the baby. Her face was scrunched as she wriggled. He had no idea how to feed her, and Norah had sailed out of the room as if that would force him to handle it. He didn't have to. He could go find Jessie or someone who knew what they were doing.

But the dog sat there, looking at him expectantly. Like he should know how to do this. Like he should handle himself, because he was the adult in the situation.

Cal frowned. He'd seen it done before. He'd watched Norah feed her. You just put the bottle in the baby's mouth. *I hope.*

He looked around the room, but the only comfortable place to sit was Norah's bed. He frowned deeper but settled himself on the edge, resting a pillow under his elbow like he'd seen Jessie and Norah do.

Then he put the bottle to Evelyn's mouth, and she immediately took it. She even grabbed it with her tiny hands. Her eyes, less sleepy now, latched on to his. Norah's eyes. A dark blue, wide and seemingly holding all the multitudes of the ocean.

He'd been so arrogant once to think he could control the universe. Marry Norah in secret. Take down a terrorist organization. Come back home and start a family even though he didn't have the faintest clue how to be a father as he'd never had one himself.

He'd thought Colonel Elliot might be a good example, except now it seemed that the man he'd admired could be…

Cal didn't know what he might be, didn't even have any clues as to *why*. Why lie? Why disappear? Why leave Norah and Evelyn unprotected?

And wouldn't that be what Cal would be doing himself if he cut all ties with them after this? It was a terrible catch-22 of leading them to danger, no matter which way he looked.

Why hadn't he had the presence of mind to think with his head instead of his heart before he'd said *I do*?

But he'd loved Norah. Painfully. With so all-encompassing a passion that even he, of the famed self-restraint, hadn't been able to control how he felt, what he wanted from Norah. And now there was a child.

His child. And she was so perfect, and looked at him, *really* looked, like she knew what he was to her. Like she understood things in the universe he never could. As if holding her here in this moment would let him in on all the secrets.

Someone cleared their throat and Cal looked up to see Dunne in the doorway, Brody behind him.

Cal had to blink, at the odd moisture in his eyes, at the pull of too many things to sort through.

"Thought you should know I asked my father, in a roundabout way, if he knew anything about Colonel Elliot's disappearance," Dunne said. His father was a contemporary of the colonel, the other superior officer who had handled their military missions as Team

Breaker, so would surely know if Colonel Elliot was missing. "Since I couldn't come out and ask without explaining why I might have heard that, I didn't get anything out of him. Either he doesn't know Elliot's missing, or he didn't want me to know."

Cal nodded, then had to clear his own throat to speak. "Hard to think of a reason he wouldn't want you to know."

Dunne shrugged. "I can't think of a reason he wouldn't know about a disappearance Norah reported to authorities."

Cal couldn't deny that.

"Landon's waiting for us in the kitchen to discuss his DC plans," Brody said.

Evelyn began making noises, and Cal realized the bottle was empty though she was still trying to suck down the last drops. He pulled the bottle from her mouth and stood. "Is Jessie around?"

"There's a little playpen thing in the living room. You can put her in there and we'll discuss Landon's plans," Brody replied.

Cal wanted to argue, but he sensed his brothers *expected* an argument, so he simply walked out of the room, Evelyn in the crook of his arm.

"You've got to burp her after a bottle," Brody said as they trailed through the kitchen and waved Landon with them to the living room. The dog followed at Cal's heels.

"You're an expert?" Cal asked, irritably.

Brody shrugged. "I read a book. Just over your shoulder and pat, pat on the back till she burps."

"Look at him. *Mr. Dad.*" Landon grinned, slapping Brody on the back.

Cal maneuvered Evelyn against his shoulder, then gave her back a few gentle pats.

"You've got to do it a little harder," Brody said when nothing happened.

"Harder? She's tiny." And so soft, so vulnerable. Where the hell had Norah gone?

Landon reached over, pushed Cal's hand out of the way, and rubbed Evelyn's back. "This is what I always saw my mother do."

Evelyn let out a barely audible pop of noise.

"Was that a burp?"

Brody shook his head, pushed Landon's hand out of the way, then gave her a few solid pats. Nothing too hard, but Cal still winced as she felt like nothing but a feather there against his shoulder.

But a surprisingly loud sound erupted from her mouth, and then she babbled happily, wriggling not in what he thought was discomfort but in a need to get moving.

"Four men and a baby," Landon said with a laugh. "We'll figure it out yet."

It was a strange sensation. The way his brothers just seemed to accept…everything. His secret marriage. This baby. When he still felt frozen in a block of ice. But Landon was joking, Brody was reading *baby* books because he was going to be a father too.

The pain in his chest was familiar. That old yearning for things he knew he couldn't have. Things that didn't belong to him. He'd always won in war, but when it came to people, he lost.

Always.

Henry put a hand on his shoulder. Gave it a squeeze. "She's a baby, not a bomb. She's yours. And she's not even a year old. You can't mess her up just yet, and you wouldn't, even if you could. But, brother, you're going to have to unclench. They're your family, just like we are."

"I know that."

"No, you want to find a way to put a wall between you and *that*, because you think it'll keep them safe. But did you think about why Norah was on that road? How she was *here*?"

"Of course I have." Not that he could explain it, but he'd had to wonder. How could he not?

"She knows. Her father knows—was one of the architects of the whole thing. Whoever put them in danger? It wasn't you. This is on them. Again."

"But I have to protect them."

"Yeah, we all will. And we'll protect each other. For the lives we're building." He pointed at Evelyn. "And I think I get it now, in a way I didn't. Why you resisted that so hard. Because you had a life before."

"It needs to stay in the before."

"Why? Because you're scared for their safety? Or because you're scared? Period."

I'm not afraid of anything. He'd said that to Norah, and he'd meant it, but he couldn't manage to say the words to Henry. Even if Henry was wrong. Of course he was scared for their safety. Why would he be scared of anything else?

He crossed to the playpen and set Evelyn down, just as Norah came down the stairs. The dog trotted over to her and she petted him, her eyes never leaving Cal's.

Her hair was wet, so she'd been upstairs taking a shower. She wore some of the new clothes Quinn and Hazeleigh had bought her. A turtleneck, likely to cover up the bruising on her neck he'd still seen so clearly this morning when he'd gone into her room.

She met his gaze, those blue eyes of hers like a window back in time. When he'd been so arrogant and sure he could make something of himself. Be a military hero, be her husband. Make everyone proud.

They said nothing—and neither did anyone else, though truth be told, Cal had forgotten about everyone else the minute she'd come down the stairs.

He itched to touch her. Press his mouth to her neck and revel in all the ways she was *alive*. Alive. And still, just the thought of any of it was a physical pain.

He'd said goodbye. Mourned…or pushed the mourning down as deep as it would go until it was almost like a dream he'd made up that she'd even existed at all.

Now she was here and she didn't remember and what was he supposed to do with that?

Because he was scared. For their safety. Of his feelings, and making all those old mistakes over and over again. Afraid she'd never remember, and he'd never know how to help her. Afraid, *petrified*, that he couldn't make this right—because he couldn't go back in time and fix the past year and a half.

"And what do we do when we're afraid, Callum?" his mother had asked him, dying there in her hospital bed. Wasting away. Him a gangly thirteen-year-old, already too well equipped to handle adult things like hospitals and medications and bills and phone calls to doctors. *"Put one foot in front of the other."* She'd said it so firmly when everything about her in the moment had been weak. *"You have so much life to live, whether I'm here or not."*

"But I want you to be here."

"I do too, but we don't always get what we want. We don't get to choose when we arrive, or when we leave, but we get to choose what we do while we're here. Never be afraid to choose."

Two days later she'd been gone. He'd been shuttled off to an aunt, then a cousin, then a group home. But he'd made his choices. He'd built himself into Cal Young, exceptional soldier. Above reproach. Phenomenal leader.

And maybe that was really what was eating away at him. It felt as though losing Norah—or thinking he had—had stripped away all those choices again. So he was a young man again, tossed from home to home, place to place, with no say in it.

Never be afraid to choose. "I fed her," he announced, into the quiet that had stretched out into discomfort. "Brody helped with the whole burping thing. I'm sure I made mistakes, but we'll get it right as we go." *One foot in front of the other.*

Norah's mouth curved ever so slightly, some of that gravity leaving her face. "I feel like it's a bit of a learning curve. Some things come instinctually, but I remember so little. Jessie's been a godsend." She moved a little closer, peered down at Evelyn in the playpen. The baby rolled and grabbed her feet, garbling happily.

Before Cal could figure out anything else to say, aside from the *I love you, I've always loved you* that wanted to escape when she didn't remember *anything*, even how to care for their daughter, there was a shout from outside. It sounded like Zara maybe, and she kept shouting. Not totally unusual.

Henry glanced out the window, then swore. "Jake's hurt."

The brothers moved immediately, pouring out the front door. Norah didn't venture outside, but stood in the doorway as they rushed to where Zara was helping Jake off a horse. The dog sat next to Norah as if watching too.

"Someone shot him," Zara said, her voice high-pitched. "We were walking the property line and he thought he heard someone and just *bang* he went down."

Jake was holding something rolled up at his side, and it was bloody. It took Landon and Henry to keep him upright once he was off the horse, Zara hovering close as they began to move him toward the house.

"Are you some kind of bullet magnet?" she said, clearly trying for humor but there were tears on her cheeks.

"Tell me what happened," Cal demanded.

Zara looked up at him and swallowed. Her hands had blood on them, and he wondered how she'd gotten Jake up on the horse, but they needed to know who before they rehashed how.

"Like I said. Soldier boy here thought he heard something, went for the tree line. Then out of nowhere, *boom*. I had my gun, but I didn't really see anyone. I heard something—saw a bit of a shadow, so I shot back," Zara said. "Maybe I hit someone, but maybe not. If I did, nothing serious, because the shooter ran. So I sure got a shot off that scared him into running."

"That's good. You did good, Zara." They'd been in the east field today. Tree line. "Brody?"

"Truck or horse?"

"I think truck, then foot. Dunne, you'll take care of Jake here. Get Quinn and or Jessie to help out. Landon and Henry, once he's settled, follow on horse. Bring the walkies." Everyone began to move. When it came to emergencies, his leadership was rarely questioned.

Until Norah trailed after him. "You're just going to...go after someone with a gun?" Norah asked, her mouth hanging open, shock radiating off her.

"I'll have one too," he replied. He grabbed the truck keys from the kitchen, then walked back through the living room. Dunne had Jake sitting down on the floor, probably because Norah and Evelyn had taken up residence in Dunne's room that also acted as medical center when necessary.

Dunne gave his verdict. "Passed through. Not as bad as the last one."

"That does not ease my concerns, Dunne," Zara said, still hovering, hands squeezed together. "Since the last one almost *killed* him."

"Almost doesn't count, Zaraleigh," Jake said, trying to smile, but he was gray and gritting his teeth.

"Don't call me that while you're bleeding out."

He reached up, winced, but took Zara's hand. "We're all right."

"We," she snorted, knuckling another tear off her cheek. She looked up at Dunne for confirmation.

"Not as bad. Promise."

Cal had to set aside the worry, because someone was out there. Someone threatened all their safety. But he knew if things were more serious, Dunne would give him *that* look. So, it was okay. It was going to be okay.

Dunne started issuing orders to Zara and Jessie, who'd just appeared, getting his supplies and creating a more sterile environment to stitch Jake up.

"I'll be back," Cal said to Norah, who was still standing there looking at a complete loss. But he didn't have time to assure her anything was okay.

He slid his cowboy hat on and went out to find the shooter.

And the dog followed at his heels.

Chapter Six

It took Norah a few minutes to get over her shock. Cal had just…disappeared outside, grim and determined, looking like some sort of Wild West hero.

Or villain, she supposed, with the gun and the dark hat.

But Brody had accompanied him. Hero, who hadn't left her or Evelyn's side, had gone with them. Quickly, after getting Jake situated, Henry and Landon had followed out the front door. Guns and hats and grim expressions.

Jessie had gone and fetched Quinn, who was now acting as Dunne's assistant of sorts. While Dunne cleaned and sewed Jake's side up right here in the living room. Zara alternately held Jake's hand and paced.

Jessie, bless her, came over to Norah. It finally broke Norah out of the reverie of shock and confusion.

"I'll take her into the kitchen," Jessie said, pointing down to Evelyn in the playpen. It was only then that Norah realized her daughter had begun to fuss. “She really liked the peaches yesterday. We’ll try those again. Sarabeth was begging me to let her try to feed her, if that’s all right? I’ll supervise, of course.”

Norah nodded. “Thank you. Really. I don’t know what I’d do…” Or what her baby would have done, without Jessie’s help these past few days. But trying to articulate that made her throat feel tight.

Jessie waved her away. “I’m happy to help. I miss this stage,” she said, reaching down and picking Evelyn up. She cuddled her to her chest. “I didn’t quite get to enjoy it when Sarabeth was little. So, I should thank you.”

Norah chewed on her lip, looking over at the door. “Aren’t you…worried?”

“About Henry, you mean?”

Norah nodded.

Jessie inhaled, seemed to think the question over. “I do often worry. It’s hardly the first time Henry’s waded into danger, but…the thing I’ve come to understand is that this is who they are. They need to face down threats or trouble. Maybe it was ingrained in them in the military—and they’re all more than capable of handling threats because of that—but I think that need to protect the little guy, fight wrong with right, is just a part of them. I think it’s what bonded them together. So, yes, of course I worry. When you love, you worry. But I also know it’s what they have to do. So I can't let that worry overwhelm my every waking moment."

Jessie looked down at where Dunne was finishing up the stitches. Jake looked more ashen than he had earlier. But it could have been so much worse. And it would have been her fault.

"Dunne was a combat medic," Jessie explained. "I can't tell you how many times Jake's been shot. Old hat for them."

Old hat. Without thinking the motion through, Norah raised her fingers to her throat. The turtleneck covered the bruises that still marred her neck, but it made her think maybe she was *old hat* too. At being hurt and victimized.

Something inside of her recoiled at the thought, but what did she know? A fat lot of nothing.

Jessie took Evelyn into the kitchen, and Norah thought she should follow, but all she could do was stare at the door. Worrying. Willing Cal and his brothers to return unscathed.

Which didn't even fully make sense. She didn't really remember anything, any connections she might have had to these men, to Cal, but the worry curled in her gut like its own weight.

Dunne, Zara and Quinn moved Jake up to his room, Jessie and Sarabeth came in and out, asking to do more things with Evelyn, and Norah just...nodded. Kate came and sat with her awhile, attempting to make conversation and get Norah to eat something, but Norah knew she didn't hold up her end of the bargain. And she couldn't stomach the thought of food when everything in her was leaden.

Because this was…connected to her. She didn't want to believe it was her fault, but it had to be, didn't it? She'd been found on their property, then someone had shown up and shot Jake. So, it was her fault. They'd been nothing but kind, generous and wonderful. And her repayment was danger and injury.

"Why don't you take this feeding, Mama?" Jessie said gently, entering the living room with Evelyn in her arms and a bottle in her hand. She transferred the baby to Norah's arms, handed her the bottle. "Then you're going to eat something."

Norah shook her head. "I can't." But she looked down at her daughter, that wave of love crashing over her as it always did. Evelyn sucked down the bottle, though her eyelids drooped more and more.

Norah realized she'd wasted a whole day sitting here worrying, while other people had taken care of her daughter, who was now just about ready to go down for the night. That much time had passed.

Jessie patted her shoulder gently. "If something had happened, we'd know by now. They're just searching for clues. For answers."

Because of me.

But Norah forced herself to smile at Jessie. "Thank you. I think it's strange to not remember anything. It's like… I can't distract myself. Because there's only the fact he—*they're* out there." *And it's because of me.*

Jessie nodded.

"But I'll feed her, put her down, then fix myself some dinner."

"There's a plate in the fridge for you. All you have to do is warm it up in the microwave. If you don't eat, we're going to have to have a long talk, missy." She waved a finger at Norah, but smiled kindly. "I've got to go wrangle my daughter into eating dinner instead of trying to dress up her cat." Jessie stood, traced her finger down Evelyn's cheek. "I'll admit, I don't know Cal very well. He keeps himself a bit apart, but I've come to think that's because a part of him was always with you."

Norah felt tears prick her eyes, though she blinked them back. She wished that were true, but he kept himself apart from her and Evelyn now that they were here. So how could what Jessie said be true? "I wish I could remember."

Jessie nodded. "You'll get there. I have faith."

"You don't even know me."

"I know you somehow fought off someone who tried to kill you, protected your baby and got to the people who could best protect you. That takes a lot of courage, and a lot of grit. You'll remember."

Norah didn't know why it steadied her. A stranger's opinion of a medical condition, when she wasn't any kind of medical professional, but Jessie's certain faith did seem to give her some strength. She fed Evelyn, burped her, then as the baby dozed, Norah got up and went to put her in the crib.

Norah turned on the baby monitor Jessie had bought for her the other day. She'd never be able to repay them all for their kindness. Never.

She went to the kitchen and warmed up the plate of food. She tried to eat. She really did. But it sat like a lump in her throat, and though she felt guilty for doing it, she scraped the food into the trash can and cleaned her dishes in the sink. All so Jessie would think she'd eaten.

You may have lost your memory, but you're still an adult who doesn't have to answer to anyone about your food intake, she lectured herself. And still felt guilty.

It wasn't late just yet, but still Cal and his brothers had been gone most of the day. What did that mean? They were out there searching for someone—and if she could only remember *something*, she could help.

She needed some air. She hooked the baby monitor receiver to her belt loop and stepped out onto the porch outside the kitchen. The sun was setting. A riot of vibrant colors against a beautiful landscape of green and pretty little ranch buildings. It was like a dream.

And someone had been out there shooting people. Because of her. What if someone had shot all four of them? And they were out there… But something in her couldn't panic at the idea. They just seemed so… strong and capable. Sure, one could get shot, hurt, when they weren't looking for trouble, but who could take down all four of them on alert?

If only she could remember. She could help. She could protect everyone. She was stronger, healing. Shouldn't she remember? The doctor had said she would.

"Worthless brain," she muttered.

"Hardly worthless."

She whirled around and saw Cal standing there inside the screen door. He opened it and Hero trotted out and over to her, stopping her from rushing to Cal. She crouched and petted the dog, then hugged him as he licked her face. How'd she get so lucky to have so many people and this dog protecting her?

She looked up at Cal, but whatever she'd been about to say died at the bleak look on his face. "You didn't find anyone." It wasn't a question. She could see it on his face.

"Some evidence someone had been walking around the property, but no. We didn't find the shooter or any clues to who it might have been, or why. Just one set of prints, so there's something positive in that."

Norah wrung her hands as she stood, and she said to Cal what she hadn't been able to say to Jessie. "This happened because of me."

"Were you out there with a gun?" Cal asked, raising an eyebrow—a very *sarcastic* eyebrow.

She didn't remember anything about this man, but she could tell he was tired. She wanted to reach out and touch his face. Run her palm down the line of his jaw, feel the scrape of the whiskers beginning to grow.

Was that a memory in and of itself? Or just basic…chemistry?

She sighed, her head beginning to pound. She wanted to rub her temples, but no doubt he'd start in on making sure she ate and rested and all that. "You know what I mean. Someone tried to kill me. Someone left me to die. Now your friend is getting shot. It's because of me. It has to be. And if I could remember any damn thing, we wouldn't be in this mess."

Cal was silent for a long moment. Because he knew she was right, *obviously.* But then he said something that made no sense. "I think we would be in this exact mess. Memory or no."

"How can you say that?" she demanded.

"I had a lot of time to think while we searched the property. About some things I'd been avoiding thinking about. But Henry pointed it out this morning and I couldn't ignore it. You were here, Norah. You shouldn't know I was here, but there's no reason you'd be here except for me. I think you fought off whoever tried to…kill you," he said, clearly struggling with the words *kill you.* "You were hurt, yes, but you fought them off and then tried to get to me. The strangulation bruises weren't fresh when I found you on the side of the road."

"So?"

"So. You fought whoever off. You got Evelyn and your dog here and got away. And you came here. I don't know how you knew to. But there's no way you were walking down a highway in Wilde, Wyoming, by happenstance. No one tried to kill you and then dumped you on the edge of my property—still alive with your baby and your dog. So, I think, whether you remember or not, you were coming here because you'd found out, because you thought I could help."

"But from everything you've told me, I had to have thought you were dead."

Cal nodded. "Three weeks ago you reported your father missing. It's possible that however that came to be, it included your father telling you I was alive. Where I was. Or you somehow finding it out on your own if he had records or something."

She suddenly felt like her legs couldn't keep her upright anymore. She sat down, right on the porch floor. Hero pressed his nose into her neck.

Cal stepped a little closer. "The bottom line is whatever this is, I think I'm connected. Not just because we were once married, but because of the old mission. Because of your father, maybe. We don't have all the pieces, but we're working on it. We'll get there."

"We'd already be there if I remembered."

He crouched next to her, and he gave Hero an absent pat, but he looked right at her. "Someone tried to kill you, Norah. Strangle you. Someone gave you that head wound. You got away. You protected your daughter and yourself. You got here. Maybe things would be simpler if you could remember, but you managed to handle all that? You don't get to give yourself a hard time for the ways your body needs to heal, okay?"

She felt that *thing* in her chest. An emotion she couldn't find the words for. One that cropped up whenever he was here. Close. Talking to her.

And he was close. Close as he'd ever allowed himself to be. Sure, he was petting Hero, but he was so near and she could just reach out. Run her palm across his jaw like she'd thought about doing. It felt... like something settled into place. The rough scrape against her palm. His dark eyes locked with hers.

He stilled. So still. While she absorbed the warmth of him, the strength of him.

A part of him was always with you. She so badly wanted that to be true in this moment. Needed to think that something about this man was connected to her more than just the daughter and history they had once shared.

He didn't pull away from her hand, and that need had built up so huge inside of her, she let whatever this feeling was propel her. Muscle memory. Real memory. Yearning. She leaned forward and pressed her mouth to his.

Maybe it was all wrong, but her entire life was *all* all wrong right now. People trying to kill her, and good people being shot. Not remembering anything, even this.

But kissing him felt right. His hand coming up to her shoulder, the gentle glide of his mouth against hers. Even the way he eased her back. It felt...safe.

She could see the hope in his eyes—the hope that she'd remembered something. Part of her wanted to lie and say she had, but honestly, she was too tired to muster the lie.

"I don't seem to remember things. Names. Events. Memories. But sometimes a feeling washes over me, and I think that might be its own kind of memory. I felt like I should kiss you, so I did."

"Ah." He was still crouching there in what could hardly be a comfortable position.

And it was all so bleak she desperately needed to lighten it. "I mean mostly I was hoping for a little Prince Charming magic, my memory magically restored."

He shook his head. "I've never been any kind of Prince Charming."

"Clearly," she said, *almost* tempted to smile. "I do feel something for you. I just don't understand it."

"You shouldn't."

"Feel it or understand it?" She shook her head and continued before he could—because she knew he'd probably say *both.* "I'm afraid you can't dictate what I feel. Even I can't do that. I know you think this is all hopeless between us, with your daughter, and maybe it is, but that doesn't change whatever feelings are here." She patted at her chest. "Even if I remembered, Callum."

He jerked, and for a moment she thought maybe *he'd* been shot.

"What did you say?" he said, his voice as raw as she'd ever heard it.

And she realized she hadn't called him Cal. That something had… She remembered this little sliver of something. "Callum. Callum, that's your full name. Callum Daniel Young." She blinked. "I remember." It was a jumble. Not a rush of everything. Just a little…blip of him. She remembered pieces of him.

Then she laughed, because…well, maybe his kiss had unlocked something after all.

Chapter Seven

Cal still crouched, though his legs were starting to fall asleep. But he was very nearly afraid he'd shatter if he moved. Break into a million pieces he was barely keeping together.

Callum. He'd stopped going by that name after his mother had died, but Norah had wheedled the information out of him the first time they'd dated, when it was supposed to be a secret fling. Nothing more than fun. Back then, she'd teased him with it. And it hadn't been until that second time, when he'd come back from some long-ago deployment he barely remembered, and hadn't been able to pretend like he'd gotten over her, that he'd told her what the name meant. He'd asked her to marry him and he'd told her his mother always called him that.

Then it had become less teasing when she said it, and more…weighty. When it mattered, she called him that.

And she'd somehow remembered. She'd *kissed* him.

All while someone was out there, taking shots at people. At his brother.

And Norah laughed, like something could be funny in this whole mess. Except she was alive. Here. Maybe remembering…something. When he didn't want to remember any of it, because he'd learned his lesson that no good came of trying to be *happy*.

Because happiness and feelings and all this didn't matter, especially when they were sitting ducks here on this porch. Even with Landon's security measures, they didn't understand the threat against them. So sitting outside was a risk they didn't need to take.

"We should go inside," he said, standing despite that pins-and-needles feelings in his legs.

Norah slowly rose. She was staring at him, but she didn't offer to say anything else.

"Landon has cameras set up all around the buildings," Cal explained. "But of course the ranch itself is too vast. So, we'll take turns keeping watch until we're sure there's no further threat."

She nodded, and when he opened the door, the dog trotted inside and Norah followed, but when he trailed behind her, she stopped. Practically boxing him in—his back to the now closed screen door, his front to her—unless he retreated back outside.

He thought about it. But in the end, he supposed he was too stubborn, too conditioned to stand up to a threat rather than retreat.

It wasn't a threat. All she did was put her hand on his chest, looking up at him like he had a million answers he knew damn well he didn't have.

Which maybe felt like a threat after all.

"Callum." She said it like she was testing the syllables on her lips. She put her palm on his jaw again, just like she used to do when she was trying to convince him he needed to relax. When she was trying to remind him there was life outside of the military and his duty.

Then she let her hand slide away, but she stepped into him, wrapping her arms around him. She leaned her head against his chest and he…

Froze. Had to. If he didn't, he'd…

"Hold me like you would if I remembered," she murmured into his chest.

Before he could stop himself, his arms came around her. It wasn't like any before time, because she felt fragile to him now. Not quite real. If he held on too tightly…

He couldn't do what needed to be done. Because there was no future here. The marriage they'd planned on died the moment a terrorist organization had his name. Norah Elliot connected to Cal Young, and so they could never, ever be connected again.

Except for this brief moment—for this period of time, to be protected against whatever was after her. He would always protect Norah and Evelyn.

But that meant, once it was safe, keeping her safe would include making her leave. Staying away from each other.

She sighed against his chest. "Is it that…you thought I was dead for so long that you had to…accept and move on? Stop loving me?" She looked up at him, and there was so much she didn't remember, but it felt like she knew more than he did.

Still, stop loving her?

Never.

He'd tried.

But in a strange way, it hadn't been all that different than losing his mother. His anchor had died, and he'd been left to drift away. But the love didn't stop. It couldn't.

He couldn't let her know that. It would make the eventuality harder. But there was heartbreak in her eyes, and she'd always been his Achilles' heel. The thing he couldn't deny. The person he couldn't lie to, no matter how hard he'd tried.

"I'll never stop," he said, the words torn from him even as he tried to push them down. But no, they came out, no matter how rusty. She didn't smile or relax, she just kept looking at him like there was more.

When he'd already told her everything he shouldn't.

"I guess I just don't understand why that hurts you," she said after a long moment that felt as though it might tear him in two.

Still, his whole life had been about putting duty ahead of pain. "Me loving you puts you in danger."

"It appears I'm already in danger," she said, pointing to the spot on her head where she had stitches, though her hair mostly covered it from the way she'd brushed it.

"You won't be in danger forever."

"But you will?"

"Yes, I will." He eased her away from him, forced himself to release her and move away. "I'm glad you remembered something. Hopefully continued rest and healing will give you back the rest of your memory, and then you'll understand."

She raised an eyebrow. "Will I?"

No, not by a long shot, but he liked the fantasy she would. "I need to go check on Jake."

She said nothing as he began to walk out of the kitchen, but the dog gave a little yip, which had Cal looking back. Her knees were giving out, and Cal managed to reach out and grab her before she fell.

"I'm okay, I'm okay," she muttered, trying to get her legs back under her. "I guess I'm a little lightheaded."

"What did you eat for dinner?" he demanded.

"Well..."

"Lunch?"

"Um."

Cal swore and settled her into a chair at the table. "You're going to sit there and eat, and I'm going to watch you swallow every bite."

CAL MOVED AROUND the kitchen while Norah watched from her seat at the table. It was an interesting sight. He moved like he was angry, like he should be banging around, but he was nearly silent as he prepared her food.

She wanted to resist out of spite, but that was stupid. Now that she knew he was safe, she did feel a little hungry, or that vague nausea that would be quelled by eating anyway. The weight in her had lifted. Maybe Jake had been shot, but she'd remembered something. Cal thought maybe this wasn't her fault…but an inevitability instead.

Her head throbbed, and she was exhausted. Hungry, obviously, though she still worried about being able to stomach whatever he put in front of her. And still, she kept reliving the way he'd said *I'll never stop.* And it had echoed inside of her, even not remembering a thing about him.

Except his full name. She'd remembered that. It had fallen out of her like a habit. Maybe she was trying too hard to remember. Maybe she needed to just…feel. And the information would come back.

Cal put a plate in front of her. It was a peanut butter sandwich. Then he put a glass of milk on the table as well. "You have to take care of yourself," he said, eyebrows furrowed in irritation.

"I tried while you were gone." She looked at the sandwich and her stomach growled. "I couldn't stomach it. Knowing I was why your friend was shot."

Cal scowled. "You're not to blame. No matter what we find out, you're not to blame for what evil men decide to do."

She supposed she couldn't argue with that, though she considered as she took a bite of the sandwich under Cal's watchful eye. She had no doubt he was going to stand there and watch her until she'd swallow every last bite just as he'd said.

It went down easier, though if she'd been left to

her own devices she wouldn't have eaten the whole thing. But Cal watched, so she ate. She drank.

Then she asked him the thing she didn't really want the answer to. "Do you think my father's one of those evil men?" She'd remembered Cal's full name, some feelings even if she didn't understand them all, but when she tried to think about her father, she could only come up blank.

Cal's expression didn't change, but she watched him carefully enough to see a certain kind of tension take up residence in his shoulders. "I don't want to think that. Your father was my mentor. I honestly thought he was one of the best men I've ever known."

"*Thought. Was.* Those are past tense."

"He told me you died while I was deployed. You weren't dead. You were pregnant. I could have…" He trailed off, his hands flexing into and out of fists even as his words came out gently.

"But you wouldn't have," she finished for him. "Because of danger. If you'd known I was alive, pregnant, you wouldn't have come home, would you? You would have left us to think *you* were dead, because that would keep us safe."

He was silent for a long, long time. Eventually, he sighed and shook his head. "I guess we'll never know what I would have done."

"I guess not." She took her last sip of milk. Would it matter? She didn't remember much of anything, but she knew somehow that you couldn't linger in what-ifs. There was only now. "Do you have any pictures of my father? Maybe something that would jog my memory?"

"I can get you some."

She nodded, then stood to take her dishes to the sink, but Cal plucked them out of her hands and went to the sink and washed them himself. She thought about what Jessie had said, about Cal and his brothers…needing to help people. Needing to stand between right and wrong.

She supposed Jessie had meant in war and random gunfire, but Norah watched Cal hand-wash a dish and glass and felt like…this was him. A man who took on responsibilities that were not his own—and that could get downright annoying. A bit of a martyr, she supposed.

But there was also something deeply *good* about it. Heroic maybe, if you didn't take it too far.

Oh, I think he probably takes it too far, she thought wryly.

And still that *feeling* deep in her chest, that yearning to go to him, intensified. She wanted to kiss him again. To whisper things about love when she still didn't fully remember loving this man.

It was somehow inside of her, though. Or had been. Maybe she'd been angry with him at the time of her injury. Maybe she'd thought he'd left her. Maybe this was some echo of something she no longer felt. Maybe when she remembered, she'd remember nothing but anger and betrayal.

But the depth and breadth of the feeling made it hard to believe it was old. Gone. Either way, she didn't *know.* And that was a frustrating, constant dull ache at the base of her skull.

She sighed. She'd remembered something. Maybe she needed to consider it a win for today and hope tomorrow yielded more. "I feel much better, thank you," she said stiffly, because if she let herself relax she might be tempted to go to him.

"Make sure you eat. All your meals," he said in return, which made her frown. She understood he was a…caretaker type, and it came with this bossy, overbearing side. Instinctually, however, she didn't care for his tone.

"And rest. We'll handle everything else. Now I'm going to go check on Jake."

She reached out and grabbed his arm before he could move past her. She frowned up at him. "I'll let you handle a lot, but not *everything else.* I want pictures of my father. I have to *try* to remember. You can't just lock me and Evelyn away until you figure this out, then ship us out when you think we're safe. We're people. Not objects."

He didn't move out of her grasp. He was so still she wasn't sure he breathed—how did he *do* that?

She could *feel* the want inside of him. He *wanted* to reach out. Hug her, maybe. Touch her definitely. And yet he held himself back. So much self-control. So much…warped sense of duty.

For a moment, so fierce and sharp, she *hated* it. And it was a familiar feeling. Even if she didn't understand it, she knew she'd felt it before. So, she didn't let go of him and she didn't stop herself from saying *her* piece.

"My daughter deserves her father, and I like to think when I remember I'll still feel that I deserve my husband. Even if I don't, the first remains true. No evil men should stop that from happening. I won't let it."

"Nor—"

"No, I need you to listen. To think about this. You're letting outside forces win, and I don't think that's you. You're letting fear win, and I know that's not you. Somehow I know that. So, you go check on Jake because you care about your friend, your *brother.* Get me the pictures and any other information about my father when you get the chance, because I have to try to help. And *you* make sure to eat and rest, because you're not a robot even if you'd like to be."

"You have the wrong expectations, Norah," he said. Sadly. *Resignedly.*

"I may not remember much, but I know you're wrong about that," she said, then turned on a heel and marched to her room. Because she wanted to cry in peace.

And then try to remember.

Chapter Eight

Cal didn't immediately go check on Jake. He was too…everything. Wound tight. Frustrated. Angry and sad. There was a thorny, desperate yearning inside of him he would damn well quash before he dealt with *anyone*.

He texted Henry he'd take over the patrol and didn't wait for Henry's response to set out. He walked around the property buildings, gun in hand, eyes on the dark, half wishing someone would jump out so he had something to fight.

But there was nothing. Nothing but the stars and his own frustration that he hadn't stopped two people he loved from getting hurt.

After an hour, Landon texted that it was his turn. Cal sighed. He didn't feel any better about the situation, but he supposed he'd walked off some of his overwhelming emotions.

When he finally got back to the main house, it was late and the house was quiet. He carefully tiptoed upstairs, and when he heard low voices coming from Jake's room he knocked on the door.

Zara opened the door and waved him in. "Come on. Revolving door."

"Sorry," Cal muttered. "Just wanted to make sure the patient is doing okay."

Jake sat in his bed, propped up on the headboard. He held a bowl and gestured with it. "Gunshot wounds equal ice cream night."

Zara leaned close to Cal and spoke in a soft whisper. "The painkillers make him a little loopy, but he's mostly fine."

Cal nodded and approached the bed.

"Here for a report, Captain?" Jake asked with a mock salute.

Cal looked back at Zara. "You sure he's all right?"

She smiled a little and nodded, then came to sit next to Jake on the bed. "Clear-headed, just goofy and thinks everything is way more funny than it is. We've been talking about what happened. What we each saw. What could have happened. Just trying to get a clear picture of it. I'm sure that's what you're here for."

It was, but something about the way she said it rankled. "And to see how he's doing."

Zara held his gaze. He wasn't sure her expression was skepticism as it was too soft, but he couldn't quite figure out what else it would be.

"Well, we both agree it certainly wasn't planned," Jake said between bites of ice cream.

"Why do you say that?"

"Everything the gunman did was…reactive, you know? I thought I saw something, so I went to investigate. *Then* he shot—or *she*, as my wife keeps pointing out. One shot. I went down. Zara shot back, and he or she bolted—hit or not, they bolted. This wasn't some planned attack, or if it was, it was really badly planned."

"We didn't find any evidence of the gunman being shot," Cal said, not sure if anyone else had transmitted the news to Jake or Zara.

"That's what Henry told me," Zara replied. "Which pisses me off."

Cal *almost* smiled. He did appreciate Zara's bloodthirsty demeanor at times.

"So, you've got someone acting alone, reacting," Jake continued. He shook his head. "I just don't think he was here to hurt anyone."

"Then why was he here?" Though Cal already had his suspicions.

"Had all the earmarking of a recon mission," Jake replied. "But you already know that."

Cal didn't respond, because yes, that was the conclusion he'd come to. And it was worse, somehow. Because recon meant an attack—a planned, careful attack, likely with more people—would come.

And they still didn't know *why*. Who? Was it about Norah? Or about Team Breaker?

"Can you sit with him for a few minutes?" Zara asked, sliding off the bed. "Dunne said not to leave him alone while he's taking the medication."

Cal nodded, but Jake grabbed Zara's hand—surprisingly quickly for a man on painkillers with a bowl of ice cream in his hands—before she could move away from the bed.

"Aren't you going to give me a goodbye kiss, wife?"

"I'm going to the bathroom, you loon," she replied, but she leaned down and pressed a kiss to his forehead. Then she rolled her eyes and disappeared.

But she was smiling. And so was Jake.

Cal couldn't help but stare at the door where Zara had disappeared. "Doesn't it…ever worry you?" He turned slowly to watch Jake's expression. Which didn't change as he ate his ice cream.

"What?" Jake replied.

Cal didn't know why he was asking such a serious question when Jake was hopped up on painkillers, but he couldn't seem to stop himself. "That we're sitting ducks. One mistake on a computer did this to us. Who's to say one mistake on a computer won't mark us again? And then Zara's marked too."

Jake seemed to consider this, as though he'd never thought of it before. "I don't worry about that."

"How can you not?"

He shrugged. "If I spent my life worrying about stuff like that, then I'd have to worry about…getting hit by a bus. Crashing my truck. Getting kicked in the head by a horse. I'd have to worry about her getting thrown and breaking her neck when she's off ranching alone. Or that one of the guys her cousin locked up over in Bent might try to target his family. You think like that, it never ends. What-ifs might not be deadly in real life like they are in war, but they sure can ruin the good parts of life you *should* enjoy." Jake sighed heavily, the spoon clattering against the now empty bowl before he set it down on the nightstand next to him—wincing a little bit, making Cal wince in return.

He'd been shot himself, once, a long time ago, but he still remembered the lingering, obnoxious pain of healing. And so much worse, he remembered when Jake had stepped in front of a bullet meant for him, almost a year ago. And watching Jake slowly heal from that, only to be here, injured again because of him.

Didn't you just lecture Norah that this isn't her fault, so it sure as hell can't be yours.

"You married her, Cal," Jake said simply. "You can't take it back."

"I'm not trying to take it back." He was thinking about her safety. Her and Evelyn's being *alive.* "There are some things in life you can't control, yes. Believe me, I'm intimately acquainted." He'd been thirteen and left with nothing, let alone any control over his life. "But there are some things you *can* and should. Norah and Evelyn need to be safe and away from any danger that might connect to me, and I can control that. I didn't understand that when I married her. Or I was too arrogant or something. But it's different now. You don't..." Cal trailed off, for a few reasons.

But Jake was Jake. "You were going to say I don't understand because Zara and I haven't jumped on the baby train yet." He laughed to himself, possibly at the term *baby train*. "Henry's there. Brody's there. Ask them, I guarantee their answers will sound like mine."

Cal looked out the window, into the dark night that surrounded the ranch. He hated that Jake was right. Hated that he felt mired in too many situations where he didn't know what to do.

"But more than that, Cal, if this is about your mom, that's not really fair to Norah *or* Evelyn."

Cal's jaw tightened. He should have known Jake would see what lay under that. He should have known he couldn't have this conversation and win.

So why did you come up here and start it?

Well, he wasn't going to stay in it. "We've got someone with a gun doing recon missions and shooting people. I don't think Landon and Hazeleigh should travel."

Jake snorted. "Good luck stopping them."

Cal sent Jake a look that would have once gotten a *yes, sir* out of him. But they weren't in the military anymore, and Jake wasn't his subordinate.

Jake's raised eyebrow and wry smile clearly said, *That doesn't work on me anymore.*

"We need more info on Colonel Elliot," Jake countered. "You know that. And if Dunne's dad wasn't giving any info, we've got to be careful. It could be pretty damn complicated. Landon and Hazeleigh will go find what they can, and we'll—or you guys, while I'm laid up—will safeguard the house and the people in it. You can brood about it, hyper focus on it, but it doesn't change anything."

Cal didn't respond. It *could* change something. If he thought of a perfect answer. If he figured out what was going on. How could he not try to change everything that was wrong? Fix it? Stop the pain and suffering and danger?

That was all he'd ever wanted to do since he was thirteen, and it had never weighed on him until…

Well, until it had all blown up in his face.

Zara returned, rolling her eyes at Jake's exuberant greeting.

"He thinks he's going to stop Landon and Hazeleigh from going to DC," Jake said, pointing in Cal's direction.

"Oh brother," Zara replied. "You're a piece of work, Cal."

"I don't understand why wanting everyone safe is me being a piece of work."

"Because you're like…trying to control everything. Like you're the smartest and best so you know what's right and no one else does."

"I do not think that," he replied, and started heading for the door. Because he wasn't in the mood for the regular programming of Cal bashing. They didn't understand—couldn't—the weight of it all.

"But you're making this about you," Zara offered, settling once again next to Jake on the bed.

Cal stopped, turned slowly. Gave Zara an icy stare that had melted stronger men than her. "Excuse me?"

She didn't melt. "And I don't just mean you. I mean all six of you."

"Hey," Jake said, frowning at her. "How's this about me?"

"Sorry, but it's true. And it's what you guys always do. I get it's a knee-jerk, because you guys were out there fighting the big bad and then you became a target. I get it. But right now, this is about Norah. Sure, you guys connect. Can't ignore that. But someone tried to *kill* Norah. So, whatever it is, even if it has to do with you, she either knows something someone doesn't want her to know—enough to kill her over. Or she pissed off the wrong imbalanced person."

"Thank you for that recap," Cal said, his words dry as dust. "I was unaware."

Zara rolled her eyes. "She thought you were dead. You thought she was dead. There's no way someone tried to kill *her* because of *you,* at least based on the information we have. So maybe you all should get your heads out of your military asses and start looking into *Norah.* Which means, Landon and Hazeleigh should go to DC and try to find out what's going on with her dad. And you, Cal, should be with Norah doing whatever you can to support her in remembering."

It wasn't new information. He understood someone had tried to kill Norah. He supposed he'd just assumed...it was about him. Which meant Zara was right on target. Which was damn annoying. "And how do you suggest I do that?" Cal returned irritably.

"I don't know Norah well enough to have specific suggestions, but you could, I don't know, *talk* to her. Be around her. Rehash your past. Not ignore her, hide from her, and otherwise act like the coward you're not."

"I am not a coward," Cal said through gritted teeth.

"I know. You're very brave and smart when it comes to men with guns and clear villains. Seen many a performance of you be all Mr. Military Man in the face of that. It's impressive. When it's the time for it. It's not the time for it now. It's time now to help Norah. And unfortunately for you both, you suck at people. You run away, because all the things you *can't* control beyond life and death scare the hell out of you." She smiled at him. Smugly. "And I can say that, because been there, done that."

Jake grinned at her. "Isn't she great?"

"Yeah, great. I'll leave you two to be great together," he muttered, and left to the sound of Jake and Zara's laughter.

Even in the midst of all *this*. He'd never understand it. Or them.

Or people.

NORAH WOKE UP to Evelyn's insistent crying. Morning light streamed in through the pretty curtains, and Norah struggled to remember what she'd been dreaming about. She sat up, massaged her forehead.

There'd been something. Something that felt important now that she couldn't access it. How frustrating.

Still, she got up and moved over to the crib. Picked up Evelyn. Instead of continuing to fuss, like she usually did, the baby cuddled into her chest and made a little, sighing sound. Then her eyes fluttered closed again.

Norah swayed back and forth as Evelyn went back to sleep, enjoying the weight and warmth of her little bundle. She returned to her bed, crawling in and enjoying the feel of her baby sleeping peacefully against her chest.

She sat there, watching the sunlight filter through the curtains, and just let herself enjoy the moment without trying to remember anything. More than sleep or even peanut butter sandwiches, this felt like the kind of rest she really needed.

She couldn't imagine anything as peaceful or wonderful as this right here.

Then she flashed back to Cal saying he'd never stop loving her.

Well, *that* wasn't peaceful. Nothing about Cal held any promise of relaxation or peace. But it still felt wonderful to know someone loved her. Particularly after thinking she'd been dead for over a year.

Someone knocked lightly on her door, and she gave a quiet *come in*. As if she'd conjured him, Cal stood there when the door opened.

"Oh... Sorry. I thought I heard her up."

"She was, but she fell back asleep, so we're just having some snuggle time."

He held a laptop under his arm, but just stood there and stared at them. Sort of like how someone might watch a train wreck. She didn't know whether to laugh or be irritated.

"Did you need something?"

That seemed to break him from his reverie. He cleared his throat and gestured to the laptop. "I have some pictures of your father and a few other things you might recognize, if you'd like to go through them."

"Yes, of course. Come in." She waved him in when he hesitated at the door. But after a few moments he stepped in and closed the door behind him. He walked slowly to her.

"She's asleep?"

Norah nodded. "She sleeps pretty soundly on me. Go ahead put the computer on my lap."

He hesitated again, this man who had absolutely *no* hesitation when leaving the house to chase down a gunman. What had life done to him to make him so afraid of or unsure of life over death? Would she remember and know, or had she never known?

He opened the laptop, brought up a picture, then set it on her lap carefully, eyeing Evelyn to make sure he didn't jostle her.

Then he stood, hands behind his back, all military stiffness. She frowned at him, not quite ready to look at the picture on the screen yet. "Are you just going to hover?"

"Would you rather I leave?" he asked, with a faint frown.

She rolled her eyes then patted the bed next to her. "Sit down, Callum."

Again, hesitation. "You don't have to keep using my full name."

Norah shrugged. "I like it."

He frowned. "I don't."

"Why not?"

His jaw tightened, and then he gingerly sat next to her on the bed, the mattress dipping with his weight. He left a healthy couple inches between them.

He did not answer her question.

Instead, he pointed to the computer screen. "This is the most recent picture of your father."

Norah turned her attention to the computer screen. A man in a military uniform filled it. He had salt-and-pepper hair, cropped short. It was hard to tell his height, but Norah didn't get the impression he was very tall. A little thick around the middle, like he'd once been fit but had maybe stopped holding himself to that high standard as middle age struck.

She felt nothing. A lump in her throat threatened to form—frustration and disappointment weaving through her hard enough to make her want to cry. But she swallowed it down. Forced away the feeling of failure. It was only the first try. "What's his name? His full name?" She'd remembered Cal's full name.

"Colonel Julian Elliot."

He may as well have said Colonel Peanut Butter Sandwich. It meant nothing to her. She sighed. "Are there others?"

"Yeah." He reached over, hit the arrow button

and the picture changed. "This one is from about three years ago."

The man was still in his military uniform, but laughing, with a drink in his hand. A more candid shot, like it was at a party or something. And he looked a little bit younger, more black than gray in his hair.

Norah stared at it, trying not to let frustration take over. "I just don't know… When I remembered your name, it wasn't like a flash. It was just…there all of a sudden."

Cal nodded. "Well, maybe you just look and you don't remember or feel anything in the moment, but at some point it'll pop up."

There was something comforting about the idea that even if these pictures didn't yield results *now*, they might still later. She hit the arrow button to the next picture.

"This one is from before you were born," Cal explained. "It's your parents' wedding photo. Colonel had a copy on his desk, and you had a copy in your apartment, so I thought maybe you'd recognize it."

It was indeed a wedding portrait. The man from the first two pictures, much younger, still in uniform. A woman in white whose face had her catching her breath.

She didn't feel some gong of recognition, but the woman—her mother—looked so much like her own reflection. Norah reached out and touched the woman's face on the screen. "I look like her, don't I?" she whispered.

"Quite a bit," Cal agreed.

"And she died? When?"

"You were seventeen."

Norah swallowed at some unknown emotion that rolled through her. Memory? Loss? Just empathizing with a younger version of herself? "How?"

Cal hesitated, and in that hesitation, Norah's stomach trembled. It would not be something as simple as a disease, or an accident. She could tell from the troubled look in his expression.

"Just tell me."

"Ah, she was..." He cleared his throat. She didn't see him move—it was stealthy or careful, but suddenly his hand was very gently on her back. Not quite a hug or having his arm around her, but still some offer of support or comfort. "Your mother was murdered."

Murdered. It hit hard, and she didn't know if it was simply the shock of it, or an echo of knowing that. "How?" she managed to ask.

"Sort of an accident, from what I was always told. There was a shooting at a place she did volunteer work at, and she was caught in the crossfire."

Norah looked at the woman in the picture. Accidentally murdered. Wrong place. Wrong time. And yet Norah couldn't access a memory of the woman or the loss of her.

She wanted to cry, but she was tired of crying. Of feeling wrung out and used up. She needed something...something to hold on to.

Callum Daniel Young. She'd remembered his

name. It was something. She had to hold on to it as a sign the rest would come.

"She's awake," Cal said, his voice rough.

Norah opened her eyes and looked down. Evelyn was squirming in her arms, but she'd reached out to Cal. Her little fingers brushing against his sleeve. Evelyn was looking at him. Her father. Not fussing to eat or be changed, just reaching out to her *father*.

Norah wouldn't let herself cry, but it was a near thing. Still, she shifted. "Here. Take her."

She knew he resisted the idea, but he didn't hesitate this time. He let Norah shift Evelyn into his arms. He looked down at her like she was some kind of alien, and Norah thought it was because the alien thing wasn't the baby, it was the feeling that washed over him. The same feeling that washed over her even when she remembered nothing.

Evelyn wrapped her little finger around Cal's, then began babbling to him.

Norah realized that for the first time, she was witnessing her child and her husband have a moment. And as much as she wanted to remember *everything*, this moment was worth all the memory loss in the world.

Chapter Nine

It was the babbling that did it. Or maybe the eye contact. The way this little girl just looked at him and spoke, even if it was gibberish to him, as if he mattered. As if he was hers.

Because he was. She had Norah's eyes, but there was something about her mouth that reminded him of his own mother. Bits and pieces of genetic material he could pick apart, but altogether she was just Evelyn.

His.

Her babbling began to get more intense, her little mouth turning into a scrunched frown, then she wriggled not from energy but from frustration.

"She needs a change and a bottle," Norah said absently, still staring at her parents' wedding photo. "Maybe some of the food Jessie bought. Could you take her to Jessie? I want to look through these again."

Cal hesitated. He'd never felt so unsure in his life, or at least not since he'd been a child. Because he knew he should keep his distance, but he couldn't seem to manage it. How did you keep someone safe and out of your personal orbit?

They were *here*. Just a few days and already knowing he'd have to send them away in the imminent future broke his heart. He'd have to give them up, *had* to, but would it really be any easier if he kept his distance? Or would he always know he'd missed this precious time with his daughter? What little there could be of it.

"I'll do it," he managed.

Norah looked up from the computer, eyebrows winging up. But she said nothing. Just watched him as he got up off the bed, Evelyn cradled in his arms. Then she turned her attention to the computer, chewing on her bottom lip, eyebrows furrowed and the echo of an old pain in her eyes.

He moved over to the makeshift changing station. He hadn't done this yet, and Evelyn wriggled and yelled her displeasure as Cal inexpertly changed her diaper. He adjusted the little self-fastener flaps once, twice, three times until it looked close to what Jessie and Norah managed.

"There are fresh clothes in that drawer," Norah said. He glanced at her and she was watching him carefully. Her expression was neutral, and that felt… painful almost.

She wasn't sure how to feel about him doing this. She wasn't sure what it meant. He should make it clear it didn't *mean* anything. Or maybe it meant everything, but it couldn't change the inevitable future.

Then she looked away, back down at the computer, and he could tell she was thinking about her mother. Her parents. Trying to remember, putting the pieces together of what he'd told her.

He hated being the one to tell her about her mother, but he would also hate for her to remember offhand, without anyone around. Something so traumatic, and awful. Something you never fully healed from.

It was what they'd first bonded over. The unfairness of it all, the uncertainty after. She'd had her father still, not been jockeyed between family and foster care, but she'd had the added complication of knowing someone else had ended her mother's life for no real reason.

For the first time, he admitted that this desperate ache inside of him wasn't just because he knew he couldn't have her, it was because he knew she didn't remember. He couldn't go and hold on to her like she remembered, like she wanted. It wasn't right when he was a stranger she only remembered vague, possibly long-gone feelings for.

Was he even the same man she'd loved? Did it matter?

He looked down at Evelyn. She wasn't crying, but she was still doing the scrunchy-faced frown like she might start any minute. He finished clumsily buttoning up her onesie—his large fingers far too big to easily snap all the tiny buttons. He lifted her to his shoulder, gave one last glance at Norah, who was still focused on the computer.

She wanted some alone time. To think. Probably beat herself up over not remembering. So, he slipped out of the room and into the kitchen.

Jessie was there, cleaning up the breakfast debris. She looked over her shoulder at him. "Oh." She said nothing else, but Cal could read the simple surprise in that one word.

He tried not to scowl. "Norah said she should eat and then have a bottle."

Jessie wiped her hands on a dishtowel then held them out. "Can do."

Cal didn't hand the baby over. "I've got it," he replied, trying to sound casual.

Jessie seemed surprised but mounted no defense and made no move to intervene, though she likely would accomplish all this better than he would.

But he was a father. As his brothers had so kindly pointed out, time and again. He couldn't undo it or run away from it. She was his duty. And as Norah had said, irritably, they weren't objects. They were people.

He settled Evelyn into the high chair, just as he'd watched Jessie and Norah and even Sarabeth do at meals. He got one of the jars of baby food. Maybe he'd kept himself apart, but he'd always been a careful observer.

And Jessie watched his every move—silently and

pretending like she was finishing cleaning, but Cal had no doubt she was ready to jump in if he faltered.

But he wouldn't. He mimicked everything he'd watched the women do, and Evelyn seemed happy to give the terrible smelling apple-carrot mush a shot.

Sarabeth clattered inside, then came to an abrupt stop, shoving something behind her back when she saw her mother.

"Sarabeth, I swear to all that is holy," Jessie said, already pointing out the door Sarabeth had just come in. "That cat has caused enough damage in this house for nine lifetimes."

Sarabeth's chin fell, then she trudged right back outside, the cat climbing up her back as she did. Cal blinked, realizing with an odd poignancy that someday, Evelyn would be just like Sarabeth. Running around. Sneaking animals into the house. Saying things to make her mother blush.

But Sarabeth's childhood had been harsh, and Cal… He had to do everything to make sure Evelyn's wasn't. That she had everything. *Everything.*

Even him.

He looked back at her, her face covered in the orange mush. Smacking happily as he brought another small scoop to her mouth.

It would be impossible for him to be around as she got older. He knew that.

But as she stared at him with her blue eyes, she looked somehow both impossibly innocent and deeper than anyone who'd only been on this planet a few months had any right to be, and it reminded him of the argument he'd had with Norah right before he'd proposed.

The argument that had made marriage and a future seem possible.

He'd tried to break up with her. He'd told her, plainly, that he didn't know how to be what she wanted. How to do a relationship. He could tell she wanted more. Weddings and babies, and it had terrified him.

If only because he'd wanted them too.

She'd turned from the sink in her tiny kitchen in her tiny apartment and pinned him with that *you are a particularly superior brand of stupid* look.

He'd seen it a few times here, even if she didn't remember. She might not have her memory, but she was still *her.*

And back then, he hadn't been so afraid to tell her bluntly. To flat out say: *"Norah, I don't know how to do this."*

"So?"

"So...so. I can't."

The silence had stretched out, so long, so piercing, he thought he was bleeding out, but he couldn't find the wound.

"Who said you have to know how to do everything?" she'd asked when she'd finally spoken.

"I always have." Because he'd had to take over when Mom had gotten sick. He'd had to figure himself out when she'd died, because no one was all that interested in helping him get there.

"No one knows everything. No one knows how to get through life. Even my father. He's Mr. Military Man now, but I saw him fall apart when my mother died. You can't control the world. You can't know how to deal with what comes at you." She'd crossed to him, where he'd sat at her table, trying to end things.

For her own good.

She'd pulled a chair over, then covered his clenched hands with hers. *"Callum, you know how to do a lot of things and I know how to handle some things and what we don't know we'll learn together."*

He'd known he shouldn't believe her, but her blue eyes had been wet and sure, and he hadn't known how to disagree with *we could do it together*, when that was all he'd ever wanted.

He'd been a different man with her. Trying to learn how to do it together.

And then she'd been ripped from him, or so he'd thought. But unlike all the other loss in his life, this one had been a lie and here she was.

Here *they* were.

They couldn't stay. Norah might be alive, but the life they'd been determined to build was still gone. He didn't know how they could stay and be safe.

What we don't know we'll learn together.

And perhaps sensing his distraction, Evelyn chose that moment to slap her hand out against the container of food and send the spoon, container and food sailing.

Then she laughed, as if it was the funniest thing in the world.

And Cal did too.

NORAH HAD A terrible headache, and still she couldn't stop. She'd begun searching the internet for information about her mother's murder. She'd found newspaper articles, and even news segments on it. She'd seen her own face, younger, in grainy pictures of the funeral.

It had happened almost a decade ago, but something about the whole thing pulled at Norah in the here and now.

Was it memory? Was it something important? But how could a ten-year-old murder, an accidental, wrong-place-at-the-wrong-time type of murder, have anything to do with…

Well, someone had tried to murder *her,* hadn't they?

But it was targeted. Probably connected to her father, and possibly connected to the military. It was desperate grasping at straws to think there'd be something here no one else had thought of.

The door eased open and Norah looked up. Cal stood there. His hair was wet and he was wearing different clothes. Instead of carrying Evelyn, he was carrying a tray.

"Evelyn decided to give us both a carrot-and-apple shower, so Jessie handled the bath because I wasn't quite sure how to manage that. I was going to have her teach me, but then I remembered you haven't eaten anything."

He set the tray down on the bed next to her—where she'd rather *he* be than a bowl of cereal, a little container of yogurt and a glass of orange juice. Still, it was a sweet gesture.

"You didn't need to wait on me."

He shrugged. "Don't mind."

He seemed different somehow. Less tense.

"I, um, hope you don't mind. I was using your computer to look up some things."

"Feel free. We've got plenty of tech around here. You can keep this one for the time being. Look up whatever you'd like. But right now, you need to eat." He reached over and took the laptop from her. He glanced at the screen before frowning and setting it down on the nightstand.

"I was looking into my mother's death. I guess that's silly. It happened so long ago."

He was still frowning, but he didn't agree with her. "It's not silly to want to understand something." He picked up the tray again, then pointedly set it on her lap. "Eat."

She tried to smile, pulled the flap back on the yogurt. "There's just something…fresh about it? I don't know how to explain it. I just had this feeling that I… That I've done this before. Looked through these articles, looking for clues. Feeling…unsettled."

Cal frowned a little, looked at the screen again. "What about it feels unsettled?"

"I don't know." She ate a spoonful of the yogurt.

"It's hard to filter through… I don't remember. Am I feeling something new? Old? Is it wrapped up in the not remembering? Is it based in reality? I can't sort through it all. I don't have enough baseline knowledge to."

Cal seemed to consider this, then carefully lowered himself onto the now empty side of the bed. He still kept inches between them, but she hadn't had to insist he sit.

"It's just, I don't remember you ever having any questions about it. Any uncertainty. It was a terrible tragedy, but not targeted or anything with questions, really."

"Exactly. Everything I read about it is so straightforward. It all makes sense. And those are facts. My feelings aren't." She really didn't want to eat, but she knew Cal would fuss if she didn't. So, she swallowed down the yogurt and moved to the cereal.

"Maybe relying on your feelings isn't the best option, but I don't think we should discount them out of hand," Cal said carefully, as if working through a very complex problem. "It's like Zara told me last night," he muttered, clearly more to himself as he pulled the laptop onto his lap and began typing away.

"What is?" she pressed.

He didn't look at her. Frowned at the article about her mother's death. "Zara said we—me and my brothers—were focusing too much on us, and I thought she meant personally, but even beyond that we're trying to tie it to the military."

"It makes sense. That's what you have in common with my father."

"But not with you. Someone tried to kill *you*." He looked at her, his gaze dropping to her neck. The bruises were almost gone now, but she would still likely put on a turtleneck once she finally got dressed. She hated that look in his eye, like somehow the marks on her were his fault.

When he'd thought she'd been *dead*.

"You think it's…separate?"

"No. I think it makes the most sense to connect to your father's disappearance. But maybe that had nothing to do with the military."

"But that doesn't explain how I got here."

"No. It's just another possibility more than an answer."

But it got her thinking about the other things that had cropped up when she'd read about her mother. "I was reading about…" She had no clear memories of her mother. Even the picture of her in the paper or the wedding photo was like looking at a stranger—sure, one that looked almost exactly like her—but a stranger nonetheless.

And still, there was this woman's voice. In her head. Norah wasn't sure, but she thought it was her mother's voice. *Good night, my darling.*

It was all so strange, so garbled and warped—memories and feelings and thoughts in the here and now.

Cal's hand came over hers. "Even if you don't remember, it's a hard thing to read about," he offered.

Because this was him too. He had all the annoying ways he wanted to take care of people, but there were also the kind ways. Like other people's anguish made him want to soothe it.

She figured that was probably one of the things she loved most about him. Who wouldn't?

"It isn't just that it was hard. It's that… All those details added up. But mine don't. When you found me in the ditch, I just had Evelyn and Hero. No phone. No ID or wallet. Mom had those things on her. I had to have had those on me at one point. Something on me to get me here. How did I get here with no cash? No phone?"

Cal stared at her for the longest time. She got the impression he was calculating things in his head. She could remember him doing that. She could recall sitting in dining rooms and her apartment—which she could remember bits and pieces of: green curtains in the living room, a picture of mountains in her bedroom. Nothing concrete, no full images. But tiny fragments of memories. Cal at her kitchen table, looking grim.

Cal, outside some building. Cold outside. Warm inside. This same look on his face.

I'm being deployed.

I guess that's it then.

I guess so.

"Cal…" She didn't know how to explain to him that she both remembered and she didn't. Flashes of things that didn't fully make sense. He'd be able to make sense of him, but there was some...need to figure them out on her own. To have her own memory fill in the blanks first.

"I don't like what I'm about to say," Cal said gruffly. "And I can't believe I'm going to say it, but time is of the essence. I think we should take Landon and Hazeleigh's place. We should be the ones who go to DC. Together."

Chapter Ten

It was a terrible idea. Cal kept trying to talk himself out of it even as he prepared to take Norah to DC.

They were keeping the reservations under Landon and Hazeleigh's names, and Landon was just switching out the ID photos. Cal didn't want anyone knowing Norah was anywhere near DC.

But she was right. All her belongings had to be somewhere. Someone had tried to kill her somewhere.

And none of those somewheres was here.

He didn't think it was DC—how had she gotten all the way here without phone, money or things for Evelyn? Add in the man who'd shot Jake, and in all likelihood it had taken place closer.

But maybe not *that* close. Because otherwise someone could have finished her off in that ditch.

Cal fought off the shudder of horror at the thought as he packed a suitcase, trying to consider what a man on vacation might pack to go somewhere.

When he'd never been on a vacation in his life.

Norah was doing the same. She'd been eager to agree to Cal's plan, far more eager than he was to put it in motion, but he knew she still had some reservations about leaving Evelyn behind.

But it was bad enough taking Norah. He'd be damned if he waltzed into danger with their baby in tow.

Theirs.

He zipped the suitcase—borrowed from Jessie, who'd been the only one between the twelve of them who had real luggage—not just duffel bags and backpacks.

He could force Norah to stay, Cal knew that, but the bottom line was that the answers, at least some of them, were there in her brain. If he took her back to her old life, her apartment, her father's house, she might remember something. Or they might find something in any of those places.

He thought about the look on her face as she'd explained what she felt over her mother's murder. Her insistence that she felt unsettled didn't sit right with Cal, even as he tried to convince himself it was just her gaps in memory causing that feeling.

She said some things were coming back to her, but mostly in such small pieces they didn't make much sense. And she had no memories of the day someone had wrapped their fingers around her throat and tried to squeeze the life out of her.

Cal paused in his packing because the red haze of fury, and utter terror at thinking about what she must have done to survive, threatened to envelope him so he was nothing but revenge.

And as much as he might want revenge with every fiber of his being, he was soldier enough to lock it away. The mission came above revenge. The truth mattered more than inflicting damage on someone.

For now.

He looked around the tiny attic room he'd taken as his from the first. Knowing he'd never want more space, or to be more comfortable, because a life without the military, without Norah, had been bleak. Why would he need space for anything else?

But now there was a woman downstairs, a baby downstairs, and he wanted more. So much more than he'd ever have the courage to articulate. But to have that more, he'd be putting them in unknown danger.

He pushed that thought aside. Maybe it'd be better to hold on to it. A reminder. A talisman, so the end of all this didn't destroy him completely.

But what did it matter if it did destroy him? His brothers had wives and girlfriends, soon-to-be children and stepchildren. He could fall apart in this little attic room and no one would know the difference.

He could be hard-ass, annoying Cal. A gargoyle or ghost or whatever he pleased once Norah was ensconced somewhere safe, in a life where she'd raise Evelyn to be a young woman. Evelyn would grow up safe and loved.

Without a father. Just like you did.

What if we learned together?

He jerked the suitcase off the bed and moved for the door.

Enough.

He had a mission to complete. No time for all the personal, painful merry-go-rounds of indecision and memory, yearning and knowing better.

Right now, the only thing he'd allow himself to think about was finding out what had happened to Norah and punish whoever had done it. Nothing else could possibly matter.

He carried the suitcase out of his room, down two flights of stairs, satisfied he'd have everything he needed.

Then he turned the corner of the bottom stairs and stopped cold. Because a few yards away, through the little doorway, he could see his family assembled in the living room. Jake sat on the armchair, Zara perched on the arm. Landon was at the little window nook, going through some papers, Dunne standing over his shoulder, while Hazeleigh sat next to him talking to Quinn.

Norah stood in the middle of the room with Evelyn in her arms. Jessie and Sarabeth were standing, making faces and noises at Evelyn, while Henry watched with a bemused expression. Brody and Kate shared secret little smiles curled up on the couch, heads together.

It stopped him cold. The whole tableau. The woman he'd once vowed to love forever, till death did them part, with his child in her arms. Like she belonged here, with the family he'd found, in this little patch of good in the middle of nowhere, Wyoming.

Right where he wanted her to be.

Then she turned a little, like she sensed him there. Her blue gaze met his, and she smiled.

They were going to find out who had tried to kill her, and still she turned to him and smiled.

Cal had never believed in miracles. Miracles would have saved his mother—or hers. It would have saved him from the hell of the ages of thirteen on. It would have stopped all the wars he'd put on a uniform to fight. Miracles didn't exist anywhere.

But she felt like one.

He didn't have the first damn clue what to do with miracles.

Norah smiling at him seemed to alert everyone else to his presence, and Landon waved him over.

"Here you go," Landon said, slapping a billfold to his chest. "ID, credit, everything you'll need. Address to Dunne's secret house."

"My father's," Dunne corrected, handing Cal a small key. "I was careful, but my father's a suspicious man. So watch your back."

Cal knew Dunne had a complicated relationship with his father, but it certainly wasn't one of hate. If Dunne's father was mixed up in this…

"I don't think he's involved, but if he is, we'll deal with it," Dunne said, his voice low. "The most important thing is the truth."

Cal didn't miss the *we*. Because the men who'd become his brothers *were* his we. No matter how they went on from this moment, or the ones before, they were linked. Always. And it wasn't just by the threat posed by a terrorist organization that might know who they were.

"I'll drive you to the airport, drop you off," Henry said. "We can bring the baby if you'd like."

Norah shook her head. "It'll be easier to say goodbye here." But she clutched Evelyn like she'd never be able to say goodbye.

"We'll take good care of her," Jessie assured her.

Norah nodded, swallowing. "I know you will. You…" She looked down at Sarabeth fondly. "You've *both* been a godsend." She kissed Evelyn's cheek, squeezed her tight, whispered goodbyes and *I love yous* to her, then turned to Cal. There were tears in her eyes, but she still smiled.

Cal didn't hesitate when Norah held Evelyn out to him. Not anymore. He took her and whispered his own goodbyes. And promises.

He'd bring her mother back and give her all the answers she deserved. Justice would be served. For both of them.

Then he handed Evelyn off to Jessie, and it was like handing a part of himself. Some long-lost part of himself he'd only just gotten back.

But there was a mystery to solve, a mess to be cleaned up, a mission to complete. He turned to Norah. "Ready?"

IT WAS SURREAL, for so many reasons, to go through the airport with Cal. to sit next to him on a plane, switch planes in Denver. to land in DC knowing this was supposed to be her home, and she felt no sense of recognition or belonging.

Which was strange, because when she looked out the window in Wyoming, something had settled inside of her like she really was home.

Or maybe it was just that without Evelyn, nothing felt like home. Jessie had been a saint and sent multiple pictures and videos, so that as they got into a car Cal had rented, Norah could go through and see her baby, healthy and loved on, perfectly happy.

Evelyn would never remember her parents had left her in Wyoming to solve her mother's attempted murder. She'd remember none of it.

Norah hoped.

They drove through different areas, and Norah searched the streetlights in the dark for some blip of memory. But she only felt out of place. Unsettled. Overwhelmed not just by the fact that she didn't remember, but at the fact there were so many lights. So many buildings and people.

"You're frowning," Cal noted, which was one of the first things he'd said to her that didn't have to do with where they were going, or what the next leg of the trip was.

She shook her head. "I'm trying to remember something. Trying to feel some sense that this is home. But all I can think is there are too many cars, too many buildings and lights. It's hard to believe I actually lived here."

He was quiet a beat, then sighed. Like she was somehow dragging what he'd say next out of him. "You weren't the biggest fan of DC. You were here because your father was, and you didn't want to abandon him after your mother died. You had someone... A great-uncle or somebody who owned a ranch in Colorado. You always said that was your dream, but you didn't want to be that far away from your father. So, it had to wait until he retired and you could convince him to move."

Norah mulled that over. This devotion to a father she didn't remember. She could picture him now, because she'd seen pictures. But there were no snippets of memory of him like there was with Cal. Even her feelings were muted. She couldn't access whatever devotion had lived inside her.

Was it the memory loss, or was it that somehow she'd lost that feeling? Was her father the reason she was in this mess? She glanced at Cal. His face seemed harder in the cool lights that played over him as they drove.

"My father was the one who told you I was dead?" she asked. He'd told her that, more than once, but she kept hoping that rehashing would unlock something inside of her. Her bruises were almost completely healed now. Why wasn't her brain?

"Yes. I..." He didn't quite fidget—Cal wasn't a man who fidgeted—but it was almost like he was tensing as if to ward off a blow. "There's no getting around the fact he lied to me. Me and my brothers had arrived at our camp, but we hadn't moved in yet. You and I had minimal communication during that time, as much as was allowed, but we were getting ready to move in and I knew I wouldn't be able to communicate with you for a while. I wanted to talk to you one more time, so I called and your father answered. I know it was him, and he said you'd been in a terrible car accident. He wasn't sure you'd make it."

Norah's stomach twisted. "You went off on your mission not knowing if I'd make it?" It seemed a terrible burden to ask of someone, even a soldier.

Cal shrugged, turning off on a more residential street. "Didn't have much of a choice."

But there was something in the way he said those words that had her pressing. "What about leave or whatever?"

Again, there was no outward response, but she could see he stiffened. "I requested it. Both then, and when I returned and got your father's message that you hadn't made it." His jaw worked, through a myriad of emotions that played out in his eyes but so quickly that she couldn't identify them all. "Both times I was denied," he said flatly.

"By my father," she clarified, though she supposed she didn't need to.

"Not directly, but I can only assume, now, that he had something to do with it."

Norah's fingers fluttered up to her neck. She had shied away from directly asking about this, because she'd been so focused on her memory. On Evelyn.

On anything but… "Do you think my father could have been the one to…"

Cal flicked her a glance, not that she could read it in the dim light of the car's interior, but he reached over. Unerringly found her hand and squeezed. "First, you reported him missing three weeks ago, so the timeline wouldn't add up. Second, he loved you. I don't have any doubts about that, Norah. Maybe he's messed up in something beyond his control, but he loved you. And I can only assume he was lying to us because he was trying to protect you."

"From what? You?"

"A family-less soldier without a cent to his name or any sort of prospects aside from dying in war? Yeah. If I had to wager a guess, he found out about us and wanted to put an end to it. But only to protect you, Norah."

She wasn't sure she believed that. What a terrible, nasty kind of protection. Selfish. If her father truly loved her, she didn't know how to believe he would have told her Cal was *dead*. Or vice versa. That wasn't love. That was control.

She closed her eyes for a moment, trying to come up with any memory of her father. A smile. A hug. A warm word. A cold one. Anything.

But there was nothing.

"This is it."

Norah opened her eyes and Cal was squinting through the dark. She didn't see anything at first, but he pulled the car into an alley and a narrow, well-kept house came into view. It was mostly in shadow, but the streetlight gave her a little glimpse. Very unassuming. There were no numbers visible, so she wasn't sure how he knew, but he no doubt did.

"I want to take a look around before we walk in. Just make sure everything is on the up and up. I think you should stay here, but..."

"But?"

"We don't know what kind of danger we're wading into here." He reached forward, pulled open the glove compartment. Inside was a gun. Norah could only blink at it. He'd rented this car form the airport. Or so she'd thought.

"How is there a gun in here? How do you *know* there's a gun in here?"

"We've got our ways," he said. "But they are ways that also might put us on the wrong person's map. So, I want you to hold on to this." He picked the gun up, then took her hand. He curled her fingers around the heavy instrument—not just handing it to her, but putting her fingers where they needed to be to shoot it.

"I'm not going to shoot someone," she said, more reflexively than because she'd thought about it. She supposed if she had gotten away from someone strangling her, she just might have shot someone or worse.

"You won't have to use it," Cal said, a soothing note to his voice. "It's just a precaution."

"Doesn't 'precaution' mean I *might* have to use it?" she demanded, not liking the feel of it at all. So heavy and cold and deadly. She would start shaking any minute—she could feel it internally already.

"Just be on the lookout. Okay? I promise, Norah, nothing is going to happen to you under my watch. If on the very slim chance someone appears, and tries to hurt you, you flick this, point, then pull that. At the very least, I'll hear the shot and come take care of it."

"What if someone tries to hurt *you*?" Norah demanded, trying desperately to sound strong to quell her panic.

Cal's mouth curved, ever so slightly. Arrogance, maybe. Probably not misplaced since he'd gone on *missions* and fought in wars and come back alive. "Just let me take a quick look around the perimeter, okay?"

When she said nothing and he just *waited* for her okay, she realized he was actually waiting for her *permission*. He wasn't going to just leave her here with a gun. He needed her to be okay with it. Which hit her harder than maybe it should have. She looked down at the gun. "Did I know how to do this before I lost my memory?"

"Yes."

She looked up at him and something about the expression on his face prompted her to ask the next question. "Was I any good at it?"

"No."

She laughed, couldn't help it. "Comforting."

He leaned forward and did something so shocking she had no words. He pressed a sweet kiss to her forehead. "Just sit tight. I'll be right back." Then he got out of the car and slid into the shadows.

Norah could only watch him go. Then look down at the gun in her hands. She didn't like the feel of it. Cold and heavy. She remained unconvinced she'd ever really learned how to use a gun. It felt so *wrong.*

And it was dark around her. How would she know what to shoot? When?

Her heart pounded, thundering in her ears. How would she possibly hear someone approach when she could only hear her own body—heartbeats and heavy breathing. She didn't want to be in the dark alone. She didn't want a gun.

Norah? Where are you? I promise, sweetheart, let's talk this out and everything will be okay.

She remembered the words—the voice here in her head—but there was only dark in her memory. And she didn't recognize the voice. It wasn't Cal, she knew that for certain. There was almost a drawl to the man's voice in her memory.

Norah, you don't understand.

Something about the words had a fury erupting inside of her. Violent and dark. But the pounding in her chest, the breath coming in pants subsided. So she could hear the quiet of the car.

She was calm now. A kind of deadly calm, one that wanted to take a shot at something, just to feel the kick of the gun.

Maybe she *didn't* want to get her memory back.

A little swath of light to the left, Cal stepping into

it. The light was from his phone. He walked to her door, then pulled it open. "Looks clear. We'll leave the suitcases but bring your purse or anything with the fake IDs on it."

Norah looked down at the gun, the way her fingers were curled around it. She didn't want to relinquish it now, which was so utterly ridiculous after not wanting to hold it in the first place.

But in a smooth, calming move, Cal took it from her. He held the car door open, waited for her to collect her things, then closed it behind her. They went up the walk with only the light of the phone.

"We'll eat. Get a good night's sleep. Start fresh in the morning," he murmured, his hand coming to rest on her back. A gentle pressure, leading her toward the door.

"We?" She asked looking up at him pointedly.

He glanced at her, the little quirk of a smile barely visible in the shadows. "I don't know what part of that 'we' you're questioning."

She didn't either. She'd meant it as…was *he* really going to rest and eat when she did? But then she started thinking about *resting* and *together.*

She probably shouldn't. What with her amnesia and all. Attempted murders and danger and being half a country away from her daughter.

But she'd kissed him, and now she wanted to know what else she was missing.

Or you want to pretend you aren't here to figure out who tried to kill *you. Pretend you didn't just re-*

member somehow you were furious at an unnamed voice in the dark.

Maybe, somehow, it was both. Pretend and yearning.

She stepped onto the little porch, but Cal stopped abruptly, his hand on her back turning into a fist in her coat, stopping her just as suddenly. He reached out with his other hand and took her arm and pulled her back to him.

“Someone’s here.” He said it so quietly she was almost convinced she’d imagined the words. But his grip on her arm was so tight she couldn’t have moved forward if she’d wanted to. “Go back to the car, Norah. Now.”

Chapter Eleven

Cal didn't watch to see if she went back to the car, but maybe he should have. There were no lights on inside the house, but he'd seen movement in the sidelight. Just a shadow, but movement was movement.

"I'm not going back to the car without you," Norah whispered behind him.

He should have known she wouldn't listen, memory or no. Not her forte.

Cal had to pretend she wasn't there and think this through. It could be innocent enough. Dunne's father kept this as a kind of safe house when he needed to put someone up. Secretly. It could just be that, although Dunne had asked his father if they could use it for a day or two. Maybe a major general didn't keep the clearest tabs on secret guests to his secret houses.

Of course a major general knows who's coming and going.

If Cal was alone, he'd sneak in and handle it. Without a second thought.

He looked back at Norah. Secreting her away in

the car didn't do much if he actually had to go in—she'd be out of sight, too far away to protect completely. He'd done a full sweep of the outside of the house and seen no signs of anyone, but that didn't mean someone couldn't arrive and attempt to hurt her.

"What if we called the police?"

He spared her a look. "This isn't quite a get-the-police-involved situation, what with fake identities and potential murderers."

Norah sighed. "Okay, it's not ideal. But I mean, we *do* have the fake identities. Couldn't we pretend like this is our rental house or whatever, and we're afraid to go in because someone's in there?"

Cal contemplated. He didn't want to get the cops involved, but the plan had some merit. It just needed a little finesse. "Here's the deal. We're going to go in. Just like this is *our* rental, like you said. You stay behind me. We'll make a lot of noise—key jiggling in the lock, chatting loudly, give whoever is in there lots of warning."

"What if whoever it is just *shoots* with all that warning?" she demanded, her whisper cracking into a bit of a shriek.

"Highly unlikely," Cal replied, though he couldn't say it was impossible. "Shooting people attracts attention. Particularly if they think we're just some lost tourists or something. Just stay behind me."

"You want me to stay behind you because they think you might shoot!"

Cal tried to bite back a sigh and tried not to wish he'd left her back in Wyoming. Where she'd be safe. Where she'd be out of the way so he could get this *done*.

But she was here, and he supposed that it should be comforting she was worried about him. Of course, she didn't remember *him*. It was very possible that at any moment she could remember everything and want to stay right here in DC. Well, not without Evelyn…

Hell, he needed to concentrate. He took her hand in his. "Trust me. Okay?"

He couldn't see in the dark, but he had no doubt she was frowning. "I mostly do. Except the part where I don't trust you not to martyr yourself to a cause, particularly when the cause is *me*."

She sounded so much like herself then. Not that she'd sounded different in the days she'd been back in his life, but the way she cut right to the heart of things, without seeming uncertain.

Yet another thing he didn't have the time to think about. "No martyrs. Just answers." He shoved the key into the lock, making as much noise as possible. "Good size," he said, putting a lot of volume and over-joviality in his voice. "I suppose we could have rented something a little smaller."

Norah sighed, but she held his hand in a death grip. "Oh, but it's nice to have the space to stretch out. Especially if we do all the sightseeing you have on your list."

He smiled in approval, then turned the key, making sure to roughly turn the knob so it made as much noise as it could. He swung the door open, let it hit the opposite wall with a thud.

"Whoops," he muttered with a chuckle. "Guess I'm a little too excited."

He stepped over the threshold, a tight grip on Norah's hand so he could keep her safely behind him. When she stepped over the threshold, she tripped loudly.

"Yikes," she said, with an overloud chuckle of her own. "It's awfully dark. I can't see a thing."

"Should be a light switch around here," Cal replied, but he took a moment to still, to listen. He watched the dark for another movement of shadow. He didn't reach for a switch, he was too busy analyzing the threat, and determining all the ways he'd keep Norah safe from it.

"Are you sure this is the right place?" Norah asked, sounding cheerful with just a touch of hesitation that suited their little charade perfectly.

"The key worked, Cheryl," Cal returned, with just enough edge to his voice to sound like some weak-willed husband.

"No need to get snippy, *Tom*," she replied, a matching edge to her own voice.

Cal nearly laughed. He slowly started to feel along the wall for the switch. He had his gun in his other hand, and though he couldn't see in the dark he knew Norah held hers as well. She was playing along just right. His only complaint was he kept having to move her behind him.

His fingers brushed the switch, but before he could flip it on, he heard the movement. It was almost a surprise, as the movement wasn't that far away and he hadn't sensed anything in his room, but Cal was ready.

Always.

He expected the swish of an arm moving a gun to aim, but it wasn't a gun or a shot, but an arm moving through the air in an attempt to land a blow. So, he didn't use his own gun in return, too risky.

Cal managed to push Norah back closer to the door they'd just entered. He ducked and narrowly dodged the blow, at the same time sweeping out a leg to kick at the attacker's leg.

The body didn't go down, but he heard the low grunt of his foot coming into contact with the attacker's shin. Now that he had a better idea of where the attacker stood and how, Cal quickly stepped forward and landed a hard blow to the man's throat.

There was a gasping, gurgling sound, then the *thunk* of the man folding, his knees hitting the ground. Cal immediately moved around to the back of the man, grabbing his arms and pulling them sharply back.

It wasn't much of a fight, which concerned Cal. Either he'd bested someone who had nothing to do with anything, or he was *meant* to best whoever this was. Still, he held the man's arms tight and did a quick sweep of the man's pockets and body to make sure he had no weapons on him.

"Get the lights," Cal said to Norah, being careful not to use her name.

He heard her moving around, likely pawing the walls for some kind of switch. When the light finally popped on, Cal had to wince as his eyes adjusted from light to dark. He could only see the back of the man's head from his angle, but still Cal knew…

He knew this man. And so did Norah.

"Colonel Elliot," he breathed out.

What the hell was Norah's *father* doing here?

NORAH STARED. It *was* the man from the pictures, though he looked older than he had in any of the photos she'd studied, looking for resemblances, memories, feelings.

He stared at her like she was a ghost. She supposed she was staring back the same way. *And* she was pointing a gun at him. She lowered it immediately.

Slowly, and with a very unreadable expression on his face, Cal dropped her father's hands. Her father got to his feet carefully, like his body hurt. He took a halting step toward her, then as if he thought better of it, looked over his shoulder at the man who'd restrained him.

The color seemed to leech out of his face. "Cal." His head whipped back to her, then to Cal again. "You…"

Cal didn't make it, Norah. I'm so sorry.

But...

It was a freak accident. No fault of his own, of course. But they're all gone. A shame. A loss for all of us.

He'd told her that. She could remember it now. Something about his voice, that look in his eyes. It brought back the scene in her mind. Her father, holding her hands, looking her right in the eye.

Lying.

"What's going on here?" Cal said, in an authoritative tone that brooked no argument.

But it clearly ruffled her father's superior military officer feathers, because some of his color returned and he straightened, smoothing out the sweater he was wearing. "I don't answer to you, Young." He turned his eyes to Norah. "Where's..."

"Where's who?" Cal returned, crossing his arms over his chest, a carefully raised eyebrow.

He was going to ask about Evelyn, but he didn't. Her father—her *father*—said nothing, wouldn't look Cal or Norah in the eye.

"I need some ice," he muttered, moving his jaw tenderly and then striding down the hallway. He flipped on lights as he went. Cal frowned after him, but didn't follow until Norah came to stand next to him.

"Any ideas?" he muttered.

Norah shook her head. She was still unsteady from the memory of her father telling her Cal was dead.

Or was it a dream? Old or new. Maybe she'd made it up in the aftermath of everything that had happened as some sort of answer.

But it seemed so clear. So real. She gripped Cal's hand, needing something to hold on to. Some steady force. "Cal…"

"Let's see what he has to say before we say anything he might overhear," he said quietly. He took her gun, and shoved it into the holster under his shirt. He kept his in his hand. Then he moved forward, pulling her along.

In the kitchen, her father stood by the freezer holding a bag of frozen vegetables to his face. When Cal and Norah entered, his eyes dropped to their hands.

He didn't sneer—in fact, nothing on his face moved at all—but there was still something about the moment that *felt* like a sneer. Like she should drop Cal's hand and step away.

But why on earth would she do that? When Cal was the one who'd found her and saved her, and she'd reported her father missing but he was *here.* Alive and well.

"I suppose Wilks gave you a key."

"Did he give *you* one?" Cal countered.

Her father said nothing to that, his mouth going into a firm line.

Norah didn't know what to think—she didn't know enough, remember enough—but she had to believe that however her father was here, Dunne's father didn't know or he would have mentioned it.

Right?

She wanted to rub her temples. None of this made sense. But Cal held on to her hand and kept with his calm but direct questioning.

"You're alive and well. Aren't you surprised to find Norah the same way?"

Her father's eyebrows drew together and he dropped the bag from his face for a minute. "What do you mean?"

Did he not know someone had tried to kill her? Or was he pretending?

Norah looked up at Cal and got the sense he had the same questions, but he didn't voice them. He didn't say anything.

Her father sighed, shoulders slumping. "Why don't we sit?" he said, gesturing to the table. Norah watched him as he lowered himself into the seat at the head of the little table. He held the bag to his cheek, but somehow...made it seem like he was in charge. While he sat there, patiently waiting for them to sit. Waiting for them to sit down and take whatever lecture he was about to give.

She recognized this man. The mantle of authority he wore as if he'd been born with it. *We'll sit. We'll talk. Because I said so. I'll sit here patiently until you're adult enough to join the conversation.*

Had he said that to her once? Surely the voices in her head were real, were memories, but it was still such a jumble. But the jumble seemed to be unraveling faster with every passing hour, with every person she connected to who she'd once known.

She remembered this man. She could picture him in a cozy little kitchen with sunlight streaming through the windows. A cold fury on his face, carefully packed away and smoothed out with a smile.

It didn't make sense, but the thing that struck her as the most concerning was that no warm feelings rushed to the surface like the days back in Wyoming with Cal. Or when she held Evelyn. There was no wave of love or yearning she didn't understand. There was no sense of safety or trust.

Only questions. Only worry.

She took a deep breath and was the first to move, first to sit. Cal followed, but she could tell it was reluctantly. He put his gun on the table in front of him, his hand resting on it. A warning, or threat, or maybe somehow both.

"All right, Elliot," Cal said, and somehow Norah knew leaving off his rank was purposeful *and* made her father mad. Though he made no attempt to express his displeasure, it was there in his shoulders. In the icy expression on his face.

For a blinding second, all Norah could think was *I have to run.* But that was… Cal had told her her father loved her. That she'd wanted to stick around DC until he retired. Her faulty memory, even as it came back to her in bits and pieces, really couldn't be fully trusted.

But haven't your feelings been on point so far?

She stared at her father, trying to get some grip on something she could trust. A fact. A full memory.

A feeling that felt good instead of uneasy. He didn't look at either of them as he sat across the table. He was organizing his thoughts, Norah figured.

She glanced at Cal. His gaze was icy as well. Everything about him was tense and coiled, ready to react. But only *react.* Not act.

And in between these two cold forces of men there was her. Uncertain. Tired. Scared.

She looked back at her father and when he finally met her gaze, she saw questions in his eyes. Uncertainties. She *knew* Cal wanted to give nothing away. But something told her…

"I don't remember anything," she said, and bit back the urge to add *or not very much.* "Cal found me, unconscious, bleeding. Someone had tried to kill me." She didn't tell him where. She didn't mention Evelyn.

She wanted to see his reaction. She wanted… No, she desperately needed to see some flare of surprise. Even if she'd question if it was good acting, she needed him to at least *act.*

His gaze turned to Cal, all accusing. "Why are you trying to lie? What is this?" He pushed back from the table, standing. "I told you to let it lie," he said, pointing at her. "What did you do?"

But Norah had no idea what she was supposed to let lie.

"What was she supposed to let lie?" Cal demanded, as if he could read her own questions, but had the strength to voice them.

She didn't feel strong. She felt weak. And like she wanted to run away and hide. Which didn't make *sense*—not with the information Cal had given her.

But maybe there was information that even Cal didn't know. "What?" Cal demanded, his voice laced with steel but none of the edgy energy pumping off her father.

"*You*, you lousy son of a bitch."

Chapter Twelve

It took Cal a full minute for those words to coalesce in his brain with any kind of understanding. "I don't know what you're talking about," he said, trying to keep his voice even. Trying to keep the crazy, wild beating of his heart under control. "You told me she was dead, and I did your bidding—in the Middle East, and when we were brought home with our fake deaths and new identities."

Colonel Elliot didn't say anymore. Cal could see a cold fury behind his gaze, but he held it under control.

Cal figured it was for Norah's sake. Not his.

"You married my daughter in secret, bad enough, but then you went ahead and left on that suicide mission."

Cal's blood ran cold. He didn't breathe for too long, and when he finally did the only thing that saved him from a gasp of pain was all the damn training he'd gone through to be prepared for the missions Colonel Elliot had sent him on.

When he spoke, it was through gritted teeth because no matter how he tried he couldn't get his jaw to relax. "We were told it was an imperative mission, and while it came with the same dangers as any other mission, it was hardly *suicide*."

Elliot scoffed. "Yes, that's why we found a bunch of soldiers who didn't have a family," he replied, as if Cal should have known all along.

And he had. He hadn't wanted to. He'd convinced himself in a million different ways they were chosen because they were good. Damn good.

But they were expendable. He'd wondered that, as his brothers had shared their childhoods and lives and what had led them there. He'd wondered if it wasn't just that no one would miss them if they were gone.

In the end, even Dunne's own father viewed them as expendable pieces to a far more important venture. Cal wished he could believe it was peace, but even now he wondered.

"But you ruined it."

"By coming back alive?" Cal returned, the bitterness leaking into his tone like acid.

"You married her," Elliot said, jerking his chin at Norah. "Left her pregnant and alone. The fact that you came back was just another step in the betrayal."

Cal shook his head. The fact Colonel Elliot could sit there, talking about suicide missions and Cal's survival like it was a *betrayal*... He didn't know how to navigate this. He wanted to cover his face with his hands, find someplace private to absorb all this.

But there was no quarter, only the pain and confusion and doing everything he could to keep it buried deep under the surface.

Elliot turned to Norah. Cal found he couldn't. He wouldn't survive whatever look was on her face.

"I did what was best, and I thought you understood that," he said to her. Earnestly. Cal had always thought Colonel Elliot doted on her. He'd loved his daughter, but there was something about the way Elliot said those words that didn't *sound* like love.

Now that Cal knew what love really was. It was what he'd felt when he thought he'd lost Norah. It was what made Jake step in front of a bullet for him last year. It was Evelyn, locking eyes with him.

It wasn't twisting things so Norah would agree with him.

Cal turned, even knowing it would hurt to look at her. She'd paled, and underneath the table her hand trembled, but she didn't let her father see that. Her chin came up. "I don't know what you're talking about. I don't remember anything."

He snorted. "Yet here you are. With him." Elliot blew out a breath, clenched his hands into fists, then relaxed them. "This isn't what's important," he said, evenly enough. "Why are you here?"

Cal could not trust this man. Ever. He never should have in the first place. Never should have idolized him or believed in him, but he had.

That was the betrayal. One he'd have to deal with later, when there weren't bigger issues at hand. He considered not telling Elliot the real reason for being here. There was no way to know what Elliot was doing, or how much he'd had to do with…anything. Maybe he was acting like he didn't know someone had tried to kill Norah.

But surely he'd figure out why they'd come all this way. Together. Without Evelyn. And if he truly didn't know about the murder attempt, maybe no matter how many betrayals there were, he could help find out who'd done it.

Can you trust this man's help?

Cal looked Elliot in the eye, icing away all the emotions that swirled deep inside of him. Focusing on the reality of this situation. The fact fury and blame were plain as day on the face of the man he'd once idolized. The fact there was an empty bottle of Jack near the sink, and the flush on Elliot's face wasn't only from exertion and anger.

This wasn't the Colonel Elliot he'd once known, so he needed to treat him like a stranger. Maybe the colonel wasn't drunk, but he'd been drinking heavily since coming here. Enough to lose some of a veneer that had always been there.

If the man was drunk enough, would he get violent? Had he? With Norah? Because of Cal. It didn't matter why. It only mattered who. So, Cal told the bare-bones truth. "Someone tried to kill Norah, and we're going to find out who."

Colonel Elliot frowned at that, eyebrows drawing together. "I don't understand why anyone would want to kill Norah," he said, rubbing at his temple with his free hand, his other occupied with the bag of frozen vegetables.

"Neither do I," Cal returned. Pointedly.

Elliot slowly lowered the bag from his face. "You think *I* had something to do with it?" he demanded.

"Someone strangled her. That's not random. That's not strangers passing. That's personal. She reported you missing over three weeks ago, and then someone tried to kill her and as far as *I* can tell, no one has reported her or Evelyn missing."

"So you know about..."

"My child? Yeah, I do." Cal had known fury before. Blinding rage and anger, but it had nothing on the full-blown realization that Elliot hadn't just caused the emotional trauma of telling them each other had died, he'd meant to deprive Cal of *ever* knowing his own child. Ever.

Norah's hand found his under the table. He couldn't unclench his fist, but it was something. An anchor, he supposed, to help remind him that his anger did nothing. His fury didn't get him back to Wyoming. Didn't keep Norah safe. Only a calm, clear mind would do that.

Elliot looked from Norah to Cal. "I don't understand any of this, but I can be certain neither do the two of you. I had to go into hiding, yes. But for military reasons that have nothing to do with Norah."

"Do they have something to do with me?"

Elliot shot him a look, and there was fury there. Hate. "You're dead, Cal. Remember?"

Which didn't answer the question, and Cal decided in this moment not to push. It would be better to have Landon poke into things without Elliot being too aware of their suspicions. Of what they knew or would know.

"Listen," Colonel Elliot said, and there was a calm now in the way he spoke that Cal remembered. It wasn't harsh or angry. It was almost kind.

Almost.

"This is a complicated and clearly confusing situation, and it's the middle of the night. No doubt you two are tired, and I need to unearth some painkillers for my jaw." He looked at Cal archly, but not with the same daggers he'd been aiming his way. "There are three bedrooms here. I suggest we all lie down for the night. Rest. In the morning, clearheaded, we can tackle this."

"Tackle *what*?" Norah asked, evidently baffled by this change in demeanor.

Cal wasn't baffled. He understood it for what it was. A tactical retreat. Not necessarily nefarious, but obviously to get a hold of his emotions. Maybe check in with anyone else involved in whatever this was. Soldiers didn't let their feelings get the better of them, and they didn't move forward without the necessary information.

Colonel Elliot had taught that to Cal himself.

"We'll tackle finding out who hurt you. Trust me, Norah. I won't rest until they're brought to justice." He said it with just the right amount of fervor.

Except…

He didn't move to touch her. Not a hug. Not a

shoulder squeeze. Not even the careful separation Cal had first employed, so sure if he touched her for anything other than basic medical care he might dissolve on the spot.

Cal had watched Colonel Elliot around Norah for *years* before this moment. He'd seen him beam at his daughter. Hug her. Carelessly sling his arm around her shoulders and talk about her as though she alone lit up the earth.

This…was different. Something had changed between them.

Yeah, she secretly married you, remember?

"*If* you're telling the truth," Colonel Elliot said, or muttered more like.

"You think I'd lie? About someone trying to *kill* me?" Norah replied, her voice raising an octave. Her outrage turned her cheeks a faint pink.

Elliot sighed. "I think he would," he said, pointing to Cal. "And I think he'd take advantage of your memory loss to make me the villain."

"You'd be wrong. Dead wrong," Norah returned, her own fury serving to level his out some.

As much as he wanted to demand answers from Colonel Elliot, Cal knew that there was no sense in fighting it here and now. It made more sense to wait. To check in with Landon and all of them back in Wyoming and figure out what was really going on.

Cal couldn't believe even now that Colonel Elliot was the one who had tried to kill Norah, but that didn't mean he hadn't done something wrong. And they needed to figure out what it was.

Soon.

"Elliot is right," Cal said, turning his hand to envelope Norah's. "We're all tired and...emotional," he said, aiming a pointed look at the man across the table. "We'll get some rest. Reconvene in the morning and try to talk this out." He held Elliot's cold gaze. *"Rationally,"* he said, with an unnecessary emphasis that had Elliot's calm demeanor tightening into something closer to rage.

"My thoughts exactly," the older man agreed icily.

NORAH WAS FROZEN. Or that was what it felt like. Ice all the way through.

Everything Cal had told her about her father did not match the man who sat across from her, at times calm and authoritative and at times seething with rage.

But at no point reaching out and touching her. At no point looking at her the way Cal had looked at her in those first days after waking up—intense, as if he was memorizing every line, shocked and surprised but *grateful* she was alive.

She trusted Cal, but none of the things he'd told her about her father made sense in this moment. Had it ever made sense? Or had something...changed?

It dawned on her then. It was Cal that had changed it. She couldn't picture it, but she remembered her father telling her Cal was dead. He'd told her that because he'd known—about the marriage, about Evelyn.

It was wrong, but that was how angry he'd been. *That* was what had changed everything.

But she didn't remember the person her father had been in the aftermath. Was it someone capable of trying to kill her?

"Norah."

It was Cal's voice. Gentle. His hand on her arm. He'd stood and she still sat at the table, staring at her father. Her father wasn't looking at her, or Cal. His gaze was kind of blank, like he wasn't staring at anything at all while he remained at the table, holding the frozen vegetables to his face.

She looked up at Cal. His expression was patient, as gentle as the hand on her arm. She sucked in a breath and let it out and then allowed Cal to draw her to her feet.

"Take your pick of rooms," her father said with a careless wave of his hand. "There are three. Everyone can have one."

It was pointed enough, Norah bristled. But Cal shook his head vaguely as if trying to impart there was no point arguing. He led her out of the kitchen, and she couldn't help the look over her shoulder.

Her father still sat at the table, drumming his fingers along the surface. His other hand held the frozen vegetables to his jaw. He was clearly lost in thought.

And not all that excited to find her alive and well. But then, maybe he hadn't known she'd been missing or hurt. Maybe he thought she or Cal was lying or exaggerating. Maybe…

But she was making excuses for a man whose behavior didn't make sense to her, and why should she do that?

She remembered him telling her Cal was dead. She remembered that. It was real. It had happened. And her father had told her a lie.

Cal led her upstairs. He poked his head into every room. There was one clearly being used—rumpled bed, clothes on a chair in the corner, one window with curtains open, one closed. A few bottles on the nightstand. Cal hesitated, then shook his head, drawing her to an empty bedroom. It reminded her of some sort of display home. Everything overmatched, in aggressively neutral shades.

Cal led her in, closed the door behind her. He gave an exaggerated yawn. "I know we don't have our things, but we can make do till morning."

"Oh. Well, I could—"

He turned abruptly, practically spinning, and he reached out and took her by the arms. Gently, yes, but then with no warning his mouth covered hers before she could say anything.

She stood there, rigid for far too long, trying to get her reeling head to make sense of any of this. She wanted to lean into it. To forget everything except the way he held her, kissed her…

But there was so much wrong, so much confusion. Then he moved his mouth to her ear.

"Don't speak. Room is bugged," he whispered, so softly it barely fluttered the strands of hair.

Bugged. Another wrench thrown into any attempt to have a clear handle on the situation. Her heart *pounded.* He thought someone was listening. Maybe even watching, by the way he fake-smiled at her.

She knew, somehow she knew, that was not Cal's real smile.

"Why?" she managed, but then shook her head. He could hardly answer.

He slowly released her, keeping that weird smile on his face. Then turned as if to survey the room, but she watched him very carefully pull his phone out of his pocket, keeping it at his side. With his other hand, he purposefully and exaggeratedly put the gun he'd still been carrying on the nightstand.

He still had the one he'd given her in the car strapped to his body and made no move to take it out of its holster.

Cal opened the closet, peered around, then moved to another door. While he moved, one hand moved over his phone without him even looking at it. He was texting, maybe one of his brothers, but didn't want to look like he was texting.

Norah started to look around the room as if maybe she could see these cameras or listening devices or whatever was supposed to be here, but Cal said her name.

"This is a bathroom," he said, gesturing at the door he'd just opened. "Why don't you clean up a little bit? Get ready for bed."

She opened her mouth to argue with him—or demand to know why he was acting so weird—but the whole someone watching or listening was reason enough, wasn't it?

So, she smiled, nodded and moved into the bathroom. She closed the door behind her. She wanted to sink into the ground and cry, but she stared straight ahead. At her reflection. At whoever Norah... Elliot or Young or whatever her last name was.

Did anything about her life make sense? Even when she remembered, would she have answers?

She closed her eyes and breathed. Maybe she didn't need answers. Being here felt like a mistake. She wanted to be back in Wyoming with her daughter. With Cal and the little family that had been built around him.

A knock sounded on the door. Then Cal's voice. "Can I come in?"

"Of course."

The door squeaked open and Cal stepped in, still smiling all *wrongly*. He left the door open. "You're exhausted, honey. Come on to bed," he said, in that overloud, fake voice. But he made hand motions toward the bath, and as confused as she felt, she finally understood.

"I just want to take a shower."

"Well, I'll join you. Saves water." He closed the door.

She sent him a baleful look, and for a moment there was almost some humor on his face.

He moved around the bathroom, looking everywhere. He turned the water on in the shower. Then pulled the curtain closed. When he spoke this time, he was dead serious, his voice just barely an audible whisper.

"No cameras in here. Bug right outside door might pick up normal voices, but whispers should be okay with the water going. Could be nothing—part and parcel with the safe house—something Dunne's father monitors if he needs to. I don't know, but I'm not about to trust it."

Or Dunne's father, Norah thought sadly. She wasn't sure if it was knowledge or just understanding that both her father and Dunne's had been Cal's heroes and now he had to suspect them, convinced they were bad men, and what a blow that would be.

Norah ran her hands over her face. "What would they be listening for?" But she knew the answer. It was the same answer for everything. *I don't know. I don't know.*

No one knew anything. Her father included.

As if he sensed her frustration, and her exhaustion, Cal reached over and gave her shoulder a squeeze. "I know that was…weird. And gave us more questions than answers, but that's an answer in of itself."

"How?"

"He's involved in something he wants to keep secret. He *hates* me. He treated you…" Cal trailed off, shook his head. "I've never seen him treat you quite like that."

"He didn't touch me," she whispered. "Shouldn't he have…hugged me? Looked at me? Assured himself I was okay?" She could still see the marks of her attack in the mirror. Shouldn't that have caused *some* reaction from her father?

Cal looked at her and she could tell he'd wondered that too, but he hesitated on agreeing with her, for whatever reason. "He was drunk," Cal mused. "Or on his way to it."

"Drunk?"

"Maybe not falling over drunk, but he's relying heavily on alcohol. There were empty bottles in the kitchen, in his room… It was on his breath, in his bloodshot eyes. Stress? Guilt? A problem no one knew about? Not sure. Too many things I don't understand."

"And I don't remember. Except…"

He looked at her expectantly. She shouldn't have said anything. It would only hurt. Didn't everything hurt enough?

"Norah."

"I just had this…flash. Not even a visual memory. All talking."

"Of?"

"Him telling me you'd died."

Chapter Thirteen

Cal had his own memory of Colonel Elliot informing him of Norah's accident and then death, so he had no doubt the man had lied to his daughter. But her remembering it was like another layer of betrayal when he was already reeling from the way his mentor had turned on him.

"In the memory, he sounds…regretful, I guess," Norah continued. "A lot of 'I'm sorries', and 'what a loss.' But I can't see it, and in a strange way it's like how he was in the kitchen just now. Like… There was an emotional reaction he should have had, but didn't."

"He knew I was alive. Which means he knew…"

Norah let her hands fall from her face and looked at him. "Knew what?"

"At that point, he knew we'd gotten married."

She nodded sadly, as if she'd already come to that realization as well. "I just don't understand why that would… If I wanted to marry you, why should it bother him?"

"I can think of quite a few reasons."

"That's your martyr complex talking," she returned, irritation simmering under all that exhaustion she was trying to battle. "But think of it from a father's perspective. I loved you."

"I had nothing when I entered the military. I was less than no one. Who would want that for their daughter? I was a soldier, with no education or experience doing something else."

"Isn't he?"

"And he probably wished he hadn't sentenced your mother to that kind of life."

"What male nonsense." She threw up her arms in disgust. "Like women don't make a choice. Like we're just purposeless beings until a man comes along to marry us and ruin us with their manly enterprises."

Cal wanted to smile because it reminded him of *her*. The *her* he'd fallen in love with. So sure of herself, the world and her place in it. Never afraid to call him out on what she'd always termed his *male* nonsense. But this was not the time or place to have this conversation, to remember old arguments. It didn't matter if it *was* nonsense, because clearly her father had felt that way enough to lie. "We'll take turns sleeping," he said, ignoring the subject altogether. "We go nowhere alone."

"Maybe if I spoke to him alone…"

"No," Cal replied, too harshly, he knew, but the

thought of Norah being alone with Elliot… "We can't be sure he didn't try to kill you."

"You said he loved me. Doted on me."

"He did. But something has changed, or he's changed. I don't trust the man who spoke to us tonight. Not with anything, including however he treated you before all this went down."

She nodded, and there was something sad in her eyes, but it wasn't disappointment at the betrayal. It was just that she understood. But she held his gaze, purposefully. "Then you have to promise not to be alone with him either."

"I promise," he agreed, if only because getting Elliot alone would mean leaving Norah alone. He wasn't about to let that happen. "What bothers me isn't just the way he spoke to you, it was the things he said too. *I did what was best, and I thought you understood that.* As though you'd had a conversation about it. As if you'd discussed it."

"If we did, I don't remember."

He rubbed her shoulder, wishing he could take that guilt away from her. She was putting too much pressure on herself. It wasn't like it was her fault she couldn't remember, but she blamed herself. "I know, but it wouldn't change anything if you did."

She clearly didn't agree with him, but she didn't argue.

"What bothered me was the *I did what was best*. Like he alone knows what's best. Better than I do. And I think he does believe that. As much as I hate to admit it, I believe he thought he did what was best. That's who he is." She said it without thinking, but something about the way she spoke made it seem like she remembered. Just like the male nonsense comment.

Cal kept still, kept silent, willing her to keep talking, hoping against hope she'd talk herself into another memory.

"He does try to do what's best, it's just… He wants what's best for *him*. It's never about me. It's my safety. My future. But isn't that just about him?" Norah frowned. "It was Evelyn."

When she fell silent, Cal tried to bite his tongue, but he couldn't manage it.

"What was Evelyn?"

"It was… I started to see him differently. The way he treated me. It wasn't love. It was control." Her frown deepened, lines digging across her forehead. "Before Evelyn, I didn't see it. He didn't want me to go out of state for college, take a job outside his office. He didn't want me talking to you or your friends. And I grew up thinking that because of how Mom died, he wanted to protect me."

Cal nodded. "That's what you always told me. That's what I always saw."

She shook her head. "But I was wrong. Naive. Blinded by love or something. And you were too, because you looked up to him. Because he said all the right things. But don't you see, he didn't *do* the right things."

Cal didn't particularly like to think back and believe he'd been wrong about everything, but he supposed it eased some of the burden that Norah had been too. They'd been young and maybe he could admit they'd been manipulated by someone who *seemed* good, because they knew how to play the role.

She sucked in a breath. "I remember… Cal, when I told him I was pregnant, he was mad."

Cal felt a new wave of fury try to spark to life, but there was already so much and he needed a cool head. "Because she was mine."

"No." She shook her head vigorously, reaching out to hold on to him. "Because pregnancy and having a child would interfere with my *duties*." She looked up at him, and her eyes were starting to get suspiciously shiny.

"Maybe—" He wanted her to take a break. To rest. To not remember if it was going to hurt. But she pressed on.

"It took me a while to untangle that. While I was pregnant, everything…soured. He had competition now—he wasn't my world. He didn't want to be a grandpa. He wanted me to do what I'd always done even when I wasn't up to it or had a doctor's appointment."

Cal should have been there. By her side. Instead, he'd gone off to fight one more mission. Needing some kind of validation that he was good enough to be her husband.

But it had been a suicide mission, and he'd been stupid enough to fall for it.

"He wanted the perfect hostess. Someone to blindly take care of all the parts of his life he didn't want to take care of. And I started to wonder if that was his objection to you too. Maybe it wasn't you, though he could certainly blame you—it was anyone who took me away from him." She sucked in a breath. "Yes, because he didn't want me to have my own place. And it was all reaching this point… I didn't want to be around him. I started… I started pulling away. Reading about toxic narcissists. He fit the bill. I just had been too young and naive to see it."

"Or he's that good at the facade. Because I would tell you that no one could ever fool me, Norah. But I thought he was…a hero. A mentor. A good man and a good father."

"My whole life. But then…" She pushed her palm to her temple. Clearly she was in pain. Pushing too hard.

"Let's go to sleep. Rest. We'll figure it all out—"

"But I want to remember it all. I want it to all come back."

"It will. With rest. Remember? The doctor said your brain is healing too. You can't push it."

She looked at him, and one of her tears escaped. "We're running out of time."

He reached out and brushed it away. "We've got time. We've got time for you not to hurt."

But there was that stubborn set to her jaw he remembered so well. He'd seen glimpses of this Norah back at the ranch, but this was full-fledged back to the woman he'd fallen in love with. Because when she wanted something, she dug in. She never gave up. And she refused to let anyone stop her. Even him.

"Here is the timeline, as I remember it," she said. Firmly. "You left... You left." She repeated it, not because she needed to but like saying it unlocked new memories. "I remember saying goodbye."

She'd cried. He'd promised her everything would work out. But it hadn't. Had it? Every promise he'd made, he'd broken—or someone had broken for him. But it didn't matter who was to blame. The result was the same.

She reached out and put her hand on his chest. "I hope you know, I understood. Even when my father told me you'd died, I understood why you'd gone. You needed to. I understood you felt like you needed to make your mark, and there was nothing else that would make you feel that." Her eyes lifted to his, a few more tears had fallen over, but he couldn't wipe them away.

He was frozen, transported to a time he'd shoved away for over a year now. "It really worked out for the best, didn't it?"

She shook her head a little. "Someone did this to us, Cal. Not you. Not me. Maybe my father, but not *only* my father. Someone went out of their way to hurt us. I want to find out who... I think..." She swallowed. "I don't have a clear memory. Maybe this is all wanting it to be true, but I think I knew. I think I'd found out something. Something someone wanted silenced."

EVEN AS NEW memories seemed to cascade inside of her, Norah struggled to think rationally. Just because something felt real, it didn't necessarily mean it was real. And some things were still fuzzy. Vague. She didn't remember marrying Cal, but she remembered saying goodbye.

Then there were feelings. Ones she couldn't articulate or maybe rationalize. And she just had this *feeling* that she'd discovered something.

But what? What could she have discovered? And why wouldn't her father mention whatever she knew. Did he not know? He'd said he thought she understood that—

"You need some sleep, Norah," Cal said gently. "Plus, we can't stay in this bathroom forever."

She looked at the shower. Steam didn't fill the small room, so clearly he hadn't put it on hot. But that did cause a problem. "If we go out with dry hair and the same rumpled clothes and someone is watching the video, they'll know we didn't take a shower."

He pulled a face, clearly irritated with the hole he'd dug himself into. "Well, we didn't bring any extra clothes, so we'll just have to get our hair wet." He took a step toward the shower, flicked the knob, then ducked his head in.

Norah rolled her eyes and looked under the sink

for towels. She found a couple of folded hand towels. She handed him one before he got out of the water.

He took it and ran it through his hair. She, on the other hand, draped one towel over her shoulders, then delicately moved her hair into the spray of the shower. She did everything she could to keep the water off her clothes.

She supposed she could have taken them off, but there was a reason they were both dancing around that subject. And it wasn't just her memory; it had to do with danger too. Besides, it was bad enough he could see the cuts and bumps and bruises on her face. The rest of her was still healing and she knew, somehow she knew, it would bury that guilt and responsibility he felt even deeper.

She pulled away, turned off the water, then worked on drying her hair enough not to drip. When she was satisfied and stood up straight, Cal smiled at her.

"See? Fresh as daisies."

She rolled her eyes, but she smiled too. He was trying to take her mind off everything, and she appreciated it. But she couldn't hold the smile for long. "Cal—"

"You're going to rest. Maybe you wake up and remember everything. Maybe it takes a while longer, but every day you're remembering more. Don't push it."

"We might be walking into something dangerous here."

"Someone tried to kill you. Someone shot Jake. At my home. It was always going to be dangerous."

"Is Wyoming really your home?"

His expression was inscrutable. But he held her gaze when he responded. "Yeah, it is."

She nodded. She knew it—didn't need her memory to see how he fit there. How, even with all his many issues, it had become his home base. The family he so sorely needed.

She didn't know what it would mean for her future if—no *when* she remembered everything, but it was good to know that he belonged there.

"Check your phone," Cal said, heading for the door. "Jessie sent you some more pictures and a video of Evelyn sleeping soundly. I don't know what those cameras can pick up, so do it in here. Call her if you need to. I'll go out and see if I can inspect the bugs a little more closely without tipping the camera off."

Norah took in a deep breath and then let it out. "Okay." But…she couldn't just let their earlier conversation go. "I need you to understand something. A parent should always want what's best for their child, and sometimes that's hard because it isn't what's best for the parent. But you loved me, Cal. And I loved you. You have always been a good man. There was no reason for him to treat you or me the way he did—no matter the reason. Don't let him make you think it was right, even if he thinks it was."

He stood very still, almost as if it took him time

to fully absorb those words. His mouth curved ever so slightly. "I married you, didn't I?"

She wished she could remember that. But she knew… "I know you said because of the whole military-faked-your-death thing we're not technically married, but I consider us technically married. You'll have to do a lot more than die on paper to get rid of me."

He looked pained, but she understood somewhere deep in her consciousness that was struggling to reassert itself that it was only because he was trying to protect her.

And possibly himself.

But whether or not she remembered the exact moment the vows were said, they had made vows to one another, and she intended to keep hers…and make him keep his.

Chapter Fourteen

Cal went into the room. He saw three bugs and suspected two camera points, but there was no real way to inspect any of them without being caught on the possible camera.

When Norah emerged from the bathroom, her hair still damp, he could tell she missed Evelyn but also was more relaxed because she'd had a chance to check on her.

Cal felt the separation himself, though he didn't understand how or why. Sure, Evelyn was his daughter, but it wasn't like he'd spent any significant time with her, and still he missed the weight of her in his arms. The way she looked at him with her mother's eyes, as though she understood far more than a baby could.

Cal sighed but forced himself to smile at Norah. "Let's hit the hay, huh?" He pulled back the covers and gestured her toward the bed. She crawled in, her eyes darting around the room. Cal killed the lights, hoping the camera didn't pick out her clearly *looking* for them.

He slid into bed next to her. She stiffened a little, but he needed to be close enough that she could hear him if he whispered. So, gingerly, he wrapped his arms around her and pulled her to him so he could settle his mouth at her ear.

It was...awkward, unlike any of the other times they'd shared a bed before. But this wasn't about... them. "I'm going to stay awake," he whispered.

"You need rest too."

"I'll get it. We'll switch. You first."

She sighed but nodded against his head. He started to release her, though some old muscle memory definitely didn't want to, but she wrapped her arms around him and held him there.

So...he didn't pull away. He kept his arms around her, his head rested on hers. They never would have slept like this before. She was a light sleeper. Fidgety. But she fell into even breathing quickly, likely exhausted from *everything.*

He held her there in the dark, and for the first time in over a year, let himself remember. As much as he still wondered how they came out of this in one piece, how they could move forward with a future together, he remembered why they'd risked it in the first place.

No matter how he'd tried to hold himself back, break it off after that first *fling* when he'd fallen for her, he hadn't been able to. Because she made him feel whole the way no one else did. It wasn't like she thought he was some paragon of virtue—which was what he'd thought she wanted—but she treated him like…someone of value. Sure, he made mistakes, and he had quirks she made fun of, or thoughts she wanted to argue with, but she listened. She cared. Sometimes, she put his needs above hers.

He didn't *want* her to, but he supposed that was love. Not wanting the other person to give things up, but wanting to do that for them, and valuing it when they did it for you.

Which made him think about what she'd said about Colonel Elliot as a father, and all the things she'd once taken at face value but had to question once she'd become a mother. And how they all landed with harsh truths he wasn't sure he was ready to face.

Because there had been something familiar about Colonel Elliot. Like some of the more problematic foster families he'd been a part of. But Colonel Elliot wore a uniform. He was a war hero. So, Cal had only sensed a familiarity, but seen the facade Colonel Elliot wanted people to see.

But underneath it all, Elliot was a man who'd always gotten his way. Who'd manipulated not just Cal, but his brothers, into going on what he now dubbed a suicide mission.

There was no thinking Cal was…well, as much as he hated to admit it, special. That was what Colonel Elliot had made him feel—special, chosen, important. It was why he'd resisted Norah as much as he could. He felt like he owed Captain Elliot for giving him the chance to be better than what he'd come from. For thinking he could be a war hero too.

But that hadn't been the hope at all. There was only hoping Cal was collateral damage. And that... that was even before Elliot had found out about him and Norah.

Cal didn't care for any of those realizations, but he had to face them. Maybe Norah would wake up remembering, but more than likely they were still in the dark. And they had to navigate whatever Colonel Elliot would bring down.

Cal knew the colonel hadn't suggested getting "rest" this evening for fun or even out of the goodness of his heart. It had been to plan, to line whatever he needed up to accomplish whatever his end goal was.

Cal watched Norah sleep and knew sleep would be impossible for him even if he tried. Later, as the sun began to rise, he slid out of bed and went into the bathroom. He checked his text messages.

From Dunne:

I checked with my father. He's being incredibly cagey—knows something. But confirmed Elliot has a key to safe house.

Cal closed his eyes, and for the briefest moment let himself...grieve, he supposed, the loss of everything he'd thought Colonel Elliot was. Maybe even Major General Wilks. If he held on to those feelings of loyalty and awe and *owing* it would cloud his thinking, and he couldn't allow that with Norah's safety in the balance.

So, he let himself accept that the men he'd idolized weren't idols. Now, it was time to figure out what to do about it.

He texted Henry, because he was afraid anyone else would beat around the bush. Any more sightings?

The response came back quickly. None. Still keeping an eye out, but seems to have left when you did.

Cal didn't think they'd been followed, but maybe it hadn't been a direct following. The fact Norah had somehow ended up at the ranch still bothered him. How had she found him? Why had she come for him?

But Zara's point kept rattling around in his head. This wasn't about *him*, even if he'd been brought into it. It wasn't even about Colonel Elliot necessarily. It was about Norah—she'd even said something about feeling as though she knew something she wasn't supposed to. She was the target, and there was no getting around it.

Which meant he knew what they had to do today.

He tucked his phone back in his pocket and was about to leave the bathroom when Norah entered. She still had bags under her eyes, but she'd gotten rest and that was what mattered.

"It's morning," she said, accusingly.

"Yeah."

"Cal, you need to—"

"I'm good. I promise." He flipped on the sink water at full blast to hopefully drown out what he was about to say. "Listen, I know what we need to do today, and I'd like to try to sneak out of here before your father wakes up. Hopefully the amount of alcohol he consumed last night means we've got a chance."

He watched her struggle with wanting to argue with him about rest, but she sighed. "What do we need to do?"

"We're going to your place."

She didn't say anything at first, but her grip on the doorknob she still held tightened. "That sounds smart." But she sounded...

"Do you not want to?"

She swallowed. "Just one of those feelings. Like it's a terrible idea. Which means it's probably our best bet."

THEY SNUCK OUT of the house like rebellious teenagers, except there was no joy in it. No freedom. Only a churning, roiling dread in Norah's gut.

Cal drove through the streets of DC, then out to the suburb where she'd been renting an apartment for a few years.

Information she didn't quite remember. She didn't even remember her address, and she thought about pointing out she didn't have keys or any way of getting in, but that was probably silly to point out to a man with Cal's skills.

He pulled into the parking lot of an apartment complex and Norah felt…nothing. The dread in her stomach remained the same as it had since Cal had told her this was the plan. It didn't dissipate, but it didn't worsen. She just felt…wrong.

Cal parked then looked at her. She knew he was searching her face not just for signs of recognition but signs of distress. He didn't want to hurt her. Didn't want her to *hurt*.

Because he loved her, and though her memories on the matter remained fuzzy in places, she knew she loved him too. Then. Now. It was who they were. Somehow.

But love didn't matter until they figured this out, because she understood this was somehow all about her, even if she didn't remember why. So, she had to put on a brave front. Act like she was perfectly happy to dive in.

Blank all that terror and dread away so Cal didn't see it. She turned to face him, tried to smile reassuringly. "Cal, I can do this."

"I know you *can*, but—"

"No. No buts. I can do it. I have to do it. If it hurts… It's only because someone tried to hurt me. At some point, that hurts whether I remember or not."

He frowned at that but nodded. They both got out of the car, and he walked over to her. He put his arm around her, guiding her to the buildings.

Nothing looked familiar, and that had her heart pounding with a different kind of nerves, but she let Cal lead her. And she tried not to lean on him too much.

"You're on the third floor," he said, nodding to a stairwell. "Apartment C."

She looked up the stairs and found herself stopping without really thinking it through. She did *not* want to go up those stairs.

But you have to. Before Cal told her they didn't have to do this—and she had no doubt that was what he was about to say—she forced herself to take the first step. Maybe it required a death grip on the railing, and a supreme amount of effort and energy, but she wasn't going to turn away.

Because, yes, the truth was going to hurt no matter what.

Cal seemed to sense she needed to lead the way, or maybe he was hoping she'd find a memory in walking there herself. But he followed, close behind as they climbed the stairs.

She looked in every corner, every shadow for some pop of memory, but there was nothing except a slight headache and vague, churning nausea. When they reached the third floor landing, Cal stopped somewhat abruptly.

She looked back at him and he glanced around, his frown deepening. "There used to be security cameras in all the outdoor hallways. I made sure of it before you took out the lease on this place. They're still on the first and second floor like before, but none here."

Dread intensified, like a heavy weight pressing

against her lungs. "Well, it suits our purposes now," Norah managed to say.

"Unfortunately, it means we can't get any footage there might have been of people coming and going." He looked at her, no doubt seeing all the swirling emotions on her face. His expression softened. "Since I don't think you've got your keys, I'll pick the lock." He bent over the knob, pulling some little tool out of his pocket and making quick work of picking the lock.

He nudged the door open slightly, peeking in. He swore. Then swung the door open the rest of the way, his gun out in his hand.

It wasn't that there was someone in there, it was that he was looking for someones in any potential corner of her trashed apartment. Because it was utterly *destroyed.* Shards of glass across the floor, things ripped off walls leaving gaping holes in the plaster. Even the TV had been knocked off its stand and lay crookedly on the floor.

Norah sucked in a breath. "Why…"

Cal crept forward. She followed, though with space between them. She doubted anyone was here. Why would they be? Was this where someone had tried to kill her? Had she made it all the way to Wyoming with her injuries?

"Stay right there," Cal ordered, then slunk into the darkened hallway.

She looked around the living room and recognized nothing. Because there was nothing *to* recognize.

The couch and chair had been slashed to ribbons. Even what had been either an end table or coffee table lay in splintered pieces next to the couch.

Cal returned from the hallway, holstering his weapon. “It’s clear, but every room is in the same shape.” He studied her face, no doubt looking for signs of recognition, but she had none.

“Who would do this?”

Cal shook his head. “Landon didn’t find any police reports. Any missing persons. Someone should have heard something, reported you missing—friends, coworkers, your father. *Someone*.”

“Maybe I didn’t have any of those things. And Dad was already supposedly missing.”

“You had friends. You had a job.”

“You don’t know. You weren’t there.”

He stiffened at that and said nothing. She sighed. She wasn’t blaming him, but she couldn’t manage his feelings right now. She couldn’t…

Her eye caught on something in the corner of the room. A little splotch of something brown. Her stomach pitched, but she felt drawn to it. Dimly, she heard Cal say her name, but something inside of her was roaring too loud to fully comprehend it.

She moved for it like she was in some sort of heavy fog. Her heart beat rapidly and her head suddenly felt too…full. There was pressure all around her. But she knew what that splotch was. She knew…

She had impressions, more than a full memory. Terror. Shadows. Crashing.

"Blood," Cal said flatly, staring down at the stain in the carpet.

Norah tried to swallow, but she couldn't... Cal's hands were on her, squeezing gently. "Norah."

But her breath was trapped in her lungs. She couldn't seem to look away from the stain. She couldn't. She couldn't...

"Breathe. Baby, you gotta breathe." He gave her a little shake. "Norah. Come on now. Breathe *in*."

He said the last so sharply it cut through some of the fog, and she managed to suck in a rattling breath. Then let it out. She focused on his hands, curled around her arms. Slowly and painfully she managed to look away from the blood, and up into Cal's face.

The memory didn't present itself in some sort of chronological, sensible fashion, but she remembered things. Bits. Pieces. They were coming together.

"It's not mine."

"What?"

"It's not my blood. Someone..." She was shaking, she realized, as Cal pulled her into him, murmuring calming things, and it helped, but no amount of reassurances took the terror away.

Someone had been in her apartment. She'd been terrified. But...not surprised. Not surprised because... "I...was looking for you."

He pulled her back enough to look at her face and she knew this would hurt him, but she couldn't not tell him. Not in the moment.

"Like, researching your death. Something... For

some reason I can't remember I was suspicious. Your death. My mother's death. I started…asking questions. Researching. And then weird things started happening."

"Okay. Okay. Don't push. Just breathe and—"

But Cal didn't finish his sentence. He dropped her and whirled in one fluid motion, gun somehow drawn without her even seeing him pull it out. But she heard the click of something, from over by the door.

"Put it down."

It wasn't Cal's voice.

Chapter Fifteen

Cal didn't drop it right away. He assessed the situation.

But the gun wasn't pointed at *him*. It was pointed at Norah. Which Cal could have handled… It was the two other men with guns behind the first that made this tricky.

"Now," the man said. He was big—dressed all in black, short military haircut. Cal didn't recognize him, and when he glanced at Norah he didn't get the feeling she did either.

All three men cocked their guns and Cal had no choice but to lower his, even as he considered all the ways he could take out all three men without Norah getting hurt.

But first he had to make sure she didn't get hurt. His best bet was to keep the men at the doorway, and his body between them and Norah.

"Drop it," the man ordered.

Cal moved a step so his body blocked Norah's. He had lowered the gun, but he hadn't let it go yet.

"We can shoot through you," the man said.

"Yeah." That they could, but if it bought him some time to set this up…

"So drop your gun now," the one in the doorway ordered. "Last warning."

Cal nodded, though he didn't immediately drop it. He bent his knees a little, giving Norah a tiny wave behind his back with his free hand that he hoped she interpreted as crouching when he did. But as he moved, and saw she was indeed crouching too, he felt something press to his back.

The gun he'd given her.

He glanced at the three men. If he shoved Norah down at the same time he whirled, he could maybe get two shots off before he got shot himself. And if he moved while he did it, he could keep it down to a nick. The third guy was the biggest problem. There'd have to be some way aside from a shot to get him to either aim poorly or not shoot at all.

He placed his gun on the floor, even as he curled his other hand around the gun Norah had given him. She was crouched behind him, so he had to act quickly before the men came closer. The minute he released the one gun, he swung the other out and shot three quick times, at the same time he gave Norah a push to the left and he swung his body to keep shielding hers.

Two men went down, and the return bullets crashed into a lamp and the window. Norah screamed, but Cal shot again, barely nicking the man still on his feet.

Then something went sailing through the air from

behind him, hitting the door so it slammed shut. Cal looked at Norah. She'd thrown a bronze vase. Perfectly.

"Good move. Out the sliding glass," he said, already pushing her toward the door that would lead them out to a little patio.

She dove for the door, scrambling to get it open, but as she stepped outside, she stopped abruptly. "We're on the third—"

He eyed the distance, then reached across to the rail of the neighbor's balcony.

"Cal."

He eyed the front door—it hadn't opened immediately. So the shots he'd got off had slowed them down. Still, it wouldn't stop them. This was the best way. The best chance to get away. He wanted to get her over first, but he could already tell she wouldn't go. He swung his leg over, held on and made the little leap, then crawled over that railing. He heard the door inside crash open.

He held out his hand. "Now."

She swallowed, and he could tell she was terrified and wanted to argue, but she took his hand.

"There's a fire escape right there." He held his hand across the small expanse between the balconies, and he didn't tell her not to look down, since no doubt she'd do it the minute he pointed it out.

"Brace yourself," he muttered, aiming his gun at the man about to come through the doorway. He shot. He didn't think he got the man—instead the man dove back inside. Norah's whole body jerked at the sound, but he kept his grip steady on her arm. "No time, Norah."

He shot at the doorway again, hoping to ward them off—but there was still the possibility one of them ran downstairs and would be waiting at the bottom of that fire escape.

Norah was shaking, but she managed to take the jump and quickly scramble over the rail. She was still shaking even on the other side, but Cal knew they didn't have time to wait for her to calm.

He shot once more, this time through the shattered glass, and managed to take the one man down. But Cal knew one man just meant the others were either going to the front—even with their injuries—or backup would.

He looked down the fire escape. So far no sign of anything, but it would be harder and take longer for them to get down than it would be for a man to run down the stairs. Backup might be far enough away they had a chance to escape. He didn't have time to weigh his options about who was better to go first. He started climbing down himself.

He could fight anyone who met them. He could help Norah if she struggled. But the man from the apartment could also follow them this way and...

He was already halfway down. Norah not far behind. He knew she was struggling—both with fear and the fact she hated heights—but she hadn't said a word. She knew this was life-and-death.

Good God, why was it life-and-death?

He hopped onto the ground and surveyed the

parking lot. More out of instinct than seeing anything, he hit the ground—a bullet narrowly whizzing by his head. "Stay right there," he yelled at Norah.

From his prone position on the ground, he got his own shot off, then rolled, so that he was hidden behind the building. "Jump off this way. Then run that way," he said pointing in the opposite direction of the shooter. "Keep the building between you and the guy."

She hesitated, but he shook his head. "Has to be this way."

She didn't like it, but she jumped off the fire escape, wincing enough to worry him, but he had to deal with the gunman before he could check how much she'd been hurt.

"Cal, we should stick together."

Cal army-crawled forward to see if the assailant had made any progress. Only a few yards away, but using cars as cover. "Just go hide behind that side of the building, okay? Please, Norah."

It must have been the *please* that did it because she nodded sharply and then ran down the length of the building.

Carefully, Cal got to his feet. He needed to get closer to the man. He needed to get some answers. Maybe they should just run, but whoever this was would only follow.

He got two quick shots off, then ran full tilt toward the car the man was hiding behind. When the man's gun came into view, Cal dove behind his own cover car.

The shot went off, the sound of it hitting the car echoing through the quiet neighborhood. This wouldn't go on much longer without interference. From other people, or the police.

Cal needed to get Norah out of here. Enough of this hiding around. He jumped the car and lunged at the shooter—who was so surprised by the brazen attack he didn't manage to turn and shoot. He just took the full weight of Cal's force.

He landed hard on the cement, and the gun came loose, clattering a few inches away from his hand. Cal managed to get a good choke hold.

"Who do you work for?" he demanded.

"The same people you do," the man gritted out. He'd been shot. Blood was seeping down a slash on his neck. It was just a graze, but it would need medical attention, and the blood loss was likely helping Cal in this fight.

He tightened his grip. "I don't work for anyone."

"That's what you think."

Cal didn't know what *any* of this meant, but he could hear sirens now. Too close. Too much potential for every kind of complication. So, Cal did the only thing he could. He took the man's gun…and ran.

Back to where Norah was hopefully waiting. Hiding. He rounded the corner. She was there, but she was not alone. She stood just a few yards from a man standing in front of a car.

Cal stopped short.

It was Major General Wilks.

Dunne's father.

And Cal didn't have the slightest idea if he could trust him or not.

The imposing man nodded toward the car. "Get in. Now."

And much to Cal's utter shock, Norah did just that of her own volition.

WHEN NORAH REALIZED Cal hadn't followed into the car at the man's command, she realized...she'd just followed a stranger's orders.

Except he wasn't a stranger. She knew him. Somehow.

She couldn't remember the details. And as she looked around the car and realized all the windows were tinted black, she had some serious reservations about whether or not she'd made the right choice. She didn't *remember,* so maybe this feeling of knowing the man was bad.

But before she could try to scramble back out of the car, Cal slid into the back with her and the man got into the driver's seat.

Cal was looking at her with a hint of disapproval, but his eyes also tracked over her like he was looking for injuries. Trauma.

"I'm all right," she said, reaching out to take his hand. She turned to the man in the driver's seat. He'd already pulled out into traffic. She could only see the back of his head and his eyes in the rearview mirror now, but she knew somehow...

"You helped me."

His eyes met hers in the mirror. "Of course I helped you."

"No, I don't… I don't think you understand." There was something at the edge of her memory, something she couldn't quite access, but she knew it was there. "I don't remember things."

His mouth pressed together. Then he gave a short nod. "We'll get somewhere safe and discuss it."

"Will we be alone in this somewhere safe?" Cal asked, distrust and disapproval dripping from his tone.

This time the man in the driver's seat turned his gaze in the mirror to Cal, briefly. "I don't know what you know, Cal, but I can see you don't trust me."

"Such a strange turn of events, Major General," Cal retorted dryly.

Major General. Another military person? She couldn't understand for the life of her why she'd been mixed up in some military thing, so that someone had tried to *kill* her. But as the man drove in silence, she realized there was something about the man's jawline, and the things she'd heard about Dunne's father being involved in Cal's military service that she put it fully together.

"You're Dunne's father."

The man sighed. "Might as well call me Owen for the foreseeable future." He flicked a glance in the mirror at Cal again. "You're not a soldier anymore, Cal. And 'Major General' or 'Dunne's father' is a mouthful."

He pulled the car into what seemed like an abandoned industrial area. Warehouses and empty parking lots and long, concrete roads leading to what appeared to be nowhere. Logically, Norah knew this should seem bad. Shady. Dangerous. But she couldn't work up the anxiety she *should* feel.

Though Cal clearly felt it enough for the both of them. He kept his hand curled around his gun, and his eyes tracked over every building they passed. When the man—*Owen*—pulled the car to a stop, he turned in his seat to face them. "Stay put. I don't want to risk anyone seeing you. I'm going to open the doors, then drive us in." He nodded to the gun Cal had. "You can keep that. I don't expect you to believe me out of hand, Cal, but I do want to help you. Sit tight."

Then he slid out of the car and walked for the door. He put a key in the lock and began the process of pulling the warehouse door back.

Norah looked at Cal. His face was stone. "Cal, I know… I know my memory is faulty, and I don't remember him…specifically. But I knew he was safe. I had the feeling I could trust him, and while I don't know if I really *can* trust my feelings, so far they haven't led me in the wrong direction."

Cal nodded. "I want to believe you. I don't think you can understand how much, but he was your father's partner in recruiting, training and sending us on our secret missions. If your father thought they were suicide missions—didn't he?"

Norah's heart sank. "It would be hard to believe otherwise." She looked out the windshield again. Owen was walking back toward the car. She shouldn't trust him. She shouldn't trust herself. But…

"I think, no matter what he might have done or not done, he wants to help now. I have to believe that."

Cal nodded sharply. "And I have to be suspicious."

She squeezed his hand. "I guess we make a good team then."

He didn't smile, but some of that tense blankness softened. Then Owen got back in the car and without a word drove it into the warehouse.

Which was when Norah realized it wasn't a warehouse. It was an airplane hangar. A small plane was parked inside.

Cal eyed it warily as Owen pulled to a stop once again.

"Private," Owen said, gesturing at the plane. "It'll get you back to Wyoming without anyone being aware you're back."

"Why would we go back to Wyoming?" Cal demanded. "A group of men just attacked us. Who claim to work for the same people *I* do, when I don't work for anyone. I'm dead."

Owen sighed. "I'll be the first to admit I don't know everything that's going on. When it comes to who attacked Norah, I'm in the dark. But I've been watching Colonel Elliot for the past month. From when Norah first came to see me, to his fake disappearance, to the moment you two showed up at my safe house—his hideout. He wants you gone, Cal. Not just fake gone. Really gone. And he's convinced a few other soldiers you're a military mission."

"Isn't that a bit extreme?" Cal returned.

"He wants them all gone," Norah said, and it was a memory. "I remember…talking with you in a room." It wasn't the whole picture. Just bits and pieces. A leather chair. Crying. A handkerchief. She looked at Owen, whose face was as impassive as Cal's. "I went to you with my suspicions. You confirmed them. We started…looking into things. His plans to erase all of you. Not fake this time. But for good." Norah felt nauseous, and her head was pounding, but she remembered it. Really remembered it. The knowledge her father was ready to kill…not just Cal, for whatever imagined betrayal was there, but all six of them.

She looked over at Cal. The color had drained from his face. Still he sat with military posture and rigid composure. He said nothing.

So, Norah said it for him. "But why?" she asked Owen.

"Let's get on the plane. We'll talk details in the air."

Chapter Sixteen

Cal had been through all manner of hells. From losing his mother, foster care, boot camp, actual war. His life had been a series of disappointments, losses and horrors.

And still he had no idea what to do with this. It was one thing for Colonel Elliot to want him dead. Insane, sure, but it at least followed some semblance of a thought process he could follow.

But all of them? His brothers. Men who'd risked their lives time and again to do good in the world.

Norah's "*But why?*" echoed in his head like a terrible earworm he couldn't get rid of. No matter how he thought of it, he couldn't work out a reason Colonel Elliot would want to erase *all* of them.

"Cal, open those doors," Owen instructed, pointing at the hangar doors that presumably led to a runway. "Norah, go ahead and climb in the plane."

"No," Cal said. He held on to Norah's hand, knowing that she'd follow orders. For whatever reason, she trusted Dunne's father, and while Cal couldn't argue with her feelings—not when they'd been right so far—he couldn't fully get on board either. "We're not separating."

Owen sighed, clearly irritated, but he didn't argue. "You were trained how to fly, right?"

Cal studied the plane. "Not one of those, but I can figure it out enough to taxi the plane to the runway."

Owen nodded. "Then you can both get in. I'll open the doors to the runway. Get the plane clear of the doorways, then I'll close up, climb in and take us up."

Cal knew they didn't have time to hesitate. If his brothers were in danger, he wanted to be boots on the ground in Wyoming, not dodging bullets in DC. But this was a gamble, and the life he was risking was Norah's.

But what other options were there? They'd been ambushed back at Norah's apartment. It had to have been at Elliot's behest. His death was some other soldier's mission now.

He pulled Norah to the plane, speaking in low tones under his breath that Owen wouldn't be able to hear as he strode in the opposite direction.

"Text Jessie. Ask about Evelyn, then say we won't be back for a few days, but we're sending a package. And say that it'll be addressed to Dunne."

"But we aren't..." Norah looked up at him. "Is that some kind of code?"

Cal nodded. "Not the sneakiest, but I think we have to be careful. I think with all this...we can't be too careful." Of course, he wasn't being careful putting all this trust in Dunne's father. Dunne had never considered his father a *bad* man, but Cal knew there was a tension there. An uncertainty. After all, his father *had* sent him into danger. Put him on their team of people without families.

Had Owen knowingly sent his son into a suicide mission? The thought filled Cal with dread and distrust.

But Norah trusted, and her feelings hadn't steered them wrong until now. She remembered Owen Wilks helping her, in a way. Surely…this was the best course of action?

Cal helped Norah into the plane while Owen walked to the back of the hangar. He began to pull back the large doors that would give the plane enough room to taxi outside.

Cal sat in the pilot's seat and studied the dash. He'd had all sorts of education in piloting the kind of transportation that could get him and his brothers out of any situation they might find themselves in.

He tested a few knobs, thought he had a handle on it enough to move the plane forward, then started the engine. He did just as Owen had instructed, taxiing the plane out of the hangar and into the sunny afternoon.

Owen closed the hangar doors, then climbed in. Cal slid out of the pilot's seat and let Owen take it. He wanted answers now, but Norah was sitting in one of the two seats in the back looking pale and worried, so he stepped back to her and took the seat next to her.

"Are we doing the right thing?" she whispered.

"We're doing the best thing," Cal replied firmly. Maybe it was the wrong choice, but he didn't have any other options. If it turned out wrong…he'd find a way to make it right.

For her.

He sat with Norah the entire long flight. When Owen brought them in for a landing, Cal could tell they were in Wyoming. Which was good. He'd at least brought them where he'd said he would.

Cal looked out the window. The runway was grass, and the small building at the end of it looked only large enough to house this one small plane.

The plane came to a stop, and then Owen slid out of his seat. "Same process. I'll open. You bring the plane in. There's a car inside."

Which all felt far too…planned. Ready.

But Cal still had his gun, and they were on his territory now. He had to trust that whatever came at them, he could handle it. He leaned toward Norah as he got up. "Text Jessie. Set your phone so she can trace your location."

Norah nodded and Cal headed for the front of the plane. He did just as before, pulling the plane into the hangar. Owen pulled the doors closed behind them and Cal turned off the plane and they got off.

There was indeed a car waiting. Cal had expected another slick, tinted-window affair—but quickly realized he should have given a major general in the military a little more credit. The windows were in fact tinted, but the vehicle was a heavy-duty truck similar to ones possessed by many landowners in the area, capable of navigating ranch work, hauling trailers and dealing with tough Wyoming winters. It would also fit right in with any other vehicles on the road, down to the Wyoming plates.

Owen held his phone in one hand, keys in the other. "Elliot's on the move, but I've got a guy following him. He took a flight to Chicago, but that might be a fake. So, we need to get to the ranch as soon as possible. It's about a forty-five-minute drive."

Owen opened the driver's door, then turned to face him and Norah. Neither one of them had made a move for the truck.

Owen was clearly at the end of his patience, but he still didn't snap, or demand compliance. He took a deep breath and explained.

"Look, when Jake got himself involved in that murder case last year, and shot in the process, I thought perhaps there needed to be a little oversight to make sure the six of you didn't end up bringing enough attention on yourselves to tie it back to your military service. But, for obvious reasons, it had to be careful, unmonitored oversight. Not on paper. Not traceable. Personal."

"Was Elliot part of this oversight?"

"At first, in the planning stages" Owen said. "But he wasn't particularly interested. I always found it odd. Until I realized…"

"Being vague doesn't help your position, Owen."

The man sighed. "I think you can understand, if you let yourself, how delicate this situation is. Elliot is a high-ranking military official. He has a lot of people working for him, doing the dirty work. In order to catch him, really catch him and have him pay, I have to have irrefutable evidence of his wrongdoing. Some of it he hasn't actually *done* yet, is just planning. Norah was helping, though, feeding me information."

Which explained why Elliot had thought she had been on his own side. Norah had been pretending.

"Helping you seems to have almost gotten her killed."

But Owen shook his head. "No, at least, not that I can prove. After Elliot disappeared, but before Norah did, Norah felt like she was in danger, which is why I was monitoring her father's every move. He did send the men who trashed her apartment, but they didn't hurt her. She wasn't there."

"What about the blood on the carpet?"

Owen sighed again. "We assumed one of the intruders injured himself with all the destruction. Norah wasn't there when it happened. She arrived home, called me and I went and investigated. I later learned it was Elliot's men, but they didn't hurt Norah. Didn't even try."

He turned to face Norah, and either he was the best actor in the world, or he was dead serious. "Whoever tried to kill you, Norah, it wasn't your father. Not unless he planned it long before I was monitoring him."

"Then who was it?" Cal demanded.

Owen shook his head, looking both resigned and

tired—two things one was *never* supposed to show in their line of work. "I don't know."

NORAH WONDERED WHAT she was supposed to feel. She supposed it should be relief her father hadn't tried to kill her…but that just meant some unknown person had put their hands around her neck and tried to squeeze the life out of her.

And she couldn't remember. She had bits and pieces now of other events from the past. But trying to bring back the moment of someone hurting her…? Nothing. Absolutely nothing.

It felt like she was floating. Untethered.

Until Cal touched her back. His hand a gentle pressure, an anchor amid all this…confusion.

"You're telling me you honestly believe Elliot wants six men he once trained dead, but he has nothing to do with the attempted murder of his daughter who was helping you investigate him of wrongdoing?"

Cal's voice was scathing, and Norah could sense Owen's impatience. Two men used to calling the shots arguing with each other when…

"It doesn't matter what he believes, or you do," Norah said, surprised at how calm her voice sounded when she wasn't even sure how she was still standing. "I want to be with my daughter now." She turned to Cal. "And you should be with your brothers. All six of you are a target, so you need to be together."

Cal looked at her in that disapproving way he had that she figured most people would read as a firm disagreement. But Norah knew, for her, he'd disapprove and do it her way anyway. It made her want to smile, lean into him. And it made her want to go home—or at least what felt like home in the midst of her fuzzy memories not all coming back—Wyoming and their daughter.

Those probably weren't the right reasons to want to go back. She should probably think about this strategically. Or lock herself in a room until she remembered everything. But Cal had been right back there—there were no *right* answers. Only next steps until they had more information.

Until she remembered. And the only thing that seemed to help her remember was to keep moving forward.

"We'll get in the car," Norah said, looking at both men, chin raised and just daring them to argue. "Owen will drive and take us through this whole mess from the beginning—leaving nothing out no matter how delicate the situation is from a military perspective. Maybe it'll jog my memory. Maybe whatever you know will help Cal connect the dots. Maybe we arrive at the ranch as in the dark as ever, but standing here disagreeing does nothing for anyone."

She looked at Owen, then Cal. She knew neither one wanted be the one to agree first. Some alpha standoff, but when she looked at Cal and gave him a significant look, he sighed. "All right," he muttered.

"Fine," Owen added.

They all got into the car together. Owen driving, Cal sliding into the back with her. They held hands, and she got the feeling he wasn't just her anchor—she was his. She remembered pieces of their life together now, and it put love into context more deeply than it had before. She *was* his anchor. They were…two pieces of a puzzle. Not perfect for one another, not without their disagreements or their jagged edges, but still the right fit.

They paused driving only for Owen to get out and close the hangar doors behind them as they left. Norah wasn't familiar enough with the area to get a good sense of where they were going or where they'd come from, so she concentrated on trying to remember the parts of what Owen told them that she'd been involved in.

"I'm not even sure what the beginning is," Owen said, and he was starting to sound tired. Like a man who'd exhausted all options.

"Was it always a suicide mission?" Cal asked.

Owen shook his head. "I know Elliot said that to you at the house. I listened to everything he said to you at the house last night. I think he even believes that, now. In a warped way, he's rewritten his own history. Because, no Cal. I didn't send you, let alone my son, on suicide missions. We definitely targeted soldiers who didn't have families, so they wouldn't have to *lie* to said families, so there wasn't an inadvertent leak. These were highly classified, intense missions and we needed men who…could give their all. Not because the six of you were expendable. You were some of the most promising soldiers across all branches we had."

Norah felt something in Cal relax. Like he'd been prepared for the worst, and she supposed he probably had been. His life had been a series of blows and worsts. When her father had called it a suicide mission...she understood how easy it probably was for Cal to believe it.

She leaned her head on his shoulder.

"There was something...off about the last mission," Owen said as he easily navigated the deserted Wyoming highway. "We'd been planning it for a few months, but suddenly Elliot wanted some changes, and to move up the timetable. I suggested caution. He threatened to go over my head."

Owen tapped his fingers against the steering wheel, but Norah kept her head on Cal's shoulder. She knew there was a thread here she needed to find, pull.

"When did you find out Cal and I had gotten married?"

Owen flicked a glance into the rearview mirror. "Not until you told me last month. Your father had never mentioned your child. He'd in fact stopped inviting me to social occasions where you might have been present. You told me that he'd encouraged you to isolate. That grieving Cal was better done in private since the missions were so secretive. So, I probably hadn't seen you in over a year when you came to my house, so early in the morning it was still dark."

Norah tried to search her memory. Heart racing.

Dark house. Nocturnal animals rustling. The sound of a dog barking somewhere in the neighborhood. Evelyn fussing in the little carrier she'd wrapped her in.

"You demanded to know where Cal was. The baby threw me at first, but I kept up with the story. He'd died in a mission last year. But then you started hammering me on dates. Exact dates. And they did not add up to what your father had told you."

"You thought I was having some sort of...grief-imposed crack with reality." She remembered the disapproval. The disbelief. But he'd also invited her in, had her take a seat on a leather chair in his living room, and handed her a handkerchief.

Owen had the good sense to look shamed. "Until you presented me with your box of evidence."

Norah couldn't remember that part.

"And a lot of your evidence matched up with when Elliot had started...acting strangely."

"Strange how?" Cal demanded.

"It wasn't in the military setting. It was more... personally. Dressed a little more, shall we say, youthful than we are. He wouldn't invite me to his home, didn't have dinners anymore, but he wanted to go out to clubs. I'd find him talking to some of the younger women at the offices in ways...well, if they'd been my daughter *I* wouldn't have been comfortable with. But it was none of my business. Look, I'm almost sixty years old. Plenty of my friends have gone through a midlife crisis. I know the signs. It wasn't any of my business."

The world around them was starting to look familiar, but Norah couldn't remember anything about a midlife crisis.

"I kept my nose out of it. But some of Norah's evidence, some of her theories, didn't connect to a midlife crisis, but they coincided with a change in behavior."

And they coincided with when Evelyn was born, Norah realized or remembered. Not just the narcissism that had come screaming back to her at the safe house, but the fact he hadn't wanted to be called *grandpa*. He hadn't wanted the reminder that he was an older man.

"The problem was, once Norah pointed some things out to me, I realized it wasn't the first time I'd seen Elliot exhibit signs of wanting to be young again."

"When was the first time?" Cal asked.

"When my mother died," Norah whispered, as a terrible thought—or memory—slammed into her. "No, *before* my mother died."

Chapter Seventeen

They were getting close to the ranch, but Cal took his eyes off the world around them to look at Norah. She'd gone pale. Her hands shook.

"He killed my mother."

Cal could only stare at her. There were denials on the tip of his tongue. Maybe Elliot was a bastard. Maybe he wanted *Cal* and his brothers dead, but surely…

"I thought she was reaching," Owen said, and again the emotion they'd both been trained to hide and push away leaked through. A sadness. A betrayal. "But the timelines all added up too perfectly. The shooter was killed by police, so no one ever got his side of the story, but the police officer who shot had a connection to Elliot. Once Norah handed me some details, I started digging into some of his confidential military files. Still, we didn't have enough evidence to go to authorities and guarantee Norah and Evelyn's safety," Owen said. "We tried, Norah and I, to find something concrete we could take to police, but we were getting nowhere. Still, in the process of this whole thing I couldn't keep lying to Norah. I finally had to tell the truth about you. It went against everything I promised myself when I set you all up in Wyoming, but… You deserved to know you were a father, Cal. And I knew I could trust Norah to handle the situation delicately, since she wanted even less than I did for you to be dead or a terrorist target."

"So, that's how she knew to find me in Wyoming, but it doesn't explain someone trying to kill her and her somehow making it here."

"No, it doesn't." Owen shook his head. "I've been trying to track down Norah for the past week. When Dunne called me about the safe house, I had hope. But this whole attempted murder thing? Sure, it makes sense to look at Elliot, but I've had tabs on his every move. His phone, his computer, his leaving the house. If he planned it, he planned it before he knew she suspected him of something, and I just don't see how that could be the case."

"What about…" Norah frowned, and a faraway look crossed her face. Cal recognized it as the one she had when she was close to a memory but couldn't quite put the pieces together to make sense of them. "There's someone else. I can… I just know…" She rubbed her temple and Cal held her closer.

"Pushing won't change it."

"Maybe it will," she replied, but she relaxed into him. "If we have all the information, we can keep everyone safe."

Cal exchanged a look with Owen in the rearview mirror. They'd both been soldiers enough to know that sometimes even having all the information didn't keep innocent people safe.

Neither of them seemed to have the words or heart to break it to Norah.

"We could drop off Cal at the ranch," Norah began, and Cal didn't even need her to say another word to know where she was going.

"No."

"Callum."

But neither his name on her lips nor the pleading look in her eye would change his mind on this. "No. We're not separating. Whatever you don't remember, it'll come back to you when your brain is ready to deal with it."

She pressed her lips together and studied him with disapproval, but he wasn't moving on that. It wasn't even ego, or the conviction that he and only he could keep her safe. It was something...far more elemental.

They'd been apart too long. Completely lost to each other—thinking the other was dead. *Dead.* They weren't going to separate and let that become a reality—for either of them.

"Let's focus on what happened here after Norah arrived," Owen said. "Dunne mentioned there was a lone shooter?"

"Yes, and no retaliation, no return since that random shot."

Owen tapped his fingers on the steering wheel

as he drove. Cal studied his profile from his spot in the back.

"But you've been watching him. You said you know his plans." Still Owen said nothing as he drove. Cal wanted to snap, but Norah's hand in his kept him dialing it back. "What aren't you telling us?" he asked.

Owen pulled his car onto the road that would lead them to the ranch. Cal was wound too tight to settle, but still it was strange how this place had come to mean *home.* It wasn't safe—Jake had been shot and Elliot knew where they were—but there was an emotional safety here. A belonging.

"Elliot was planning some kind of diversion. That would draw the six of you out of the house, so there wouldn't be…collateral damage. He hadn't worked it out yet. I don't know for sure the man who shot Jake worked for Elliot, but I do know he was trying to get a sense of the terrain, the layout, to enact his plan."

Cal had to carefully breathe through the white-hot rage that spread through him. That his wife, his daughter, his friends could be considered *collateral damage…*

"I suppose it's something," Owen offered. "The women and children will be safe, and—"

"No. Only *some* of the women and children. Someone still tried to kill Norah. They tried to *strangle* her. If this doesn't connect to Elliot, we have *two* threats."

Owen pulled to a stop in front of the house that had become home. "Yes, we do. But on the bright side, we have seven military minds to put together and figure out how to protect all of you." Owen looked back at them. "I promise you, this will be over. Whatever it takes, we'll put an end to it. I'm sorry it went on this long. And I'm sorry, Norah, that I didn't react as quickly as I should have. Sometimes feelings get in the way of what's right."

Norah leaned forward and touched Owen's shoulder. "Owen, I don't remember everything, but I know you've gone above and beyond in trying to help Evelyn and me. You're the reason I know Cal's alive. I understand now, probably in a way I didn't when you told me, how much that must have cost you to tell me, and how much trust you put in me by telling me. Not just Cal's life, but your son's. So, no matter what, I owe you."

Cal still held Norah's hand and watched her and the way her words loosened the tenseness in Owen's shoulders.

It was one of the many reasons he'd fallen in love with her. Not just her kindness, but the way she wielded it. He'd never known anyone who could just tap into an endless well of *goodness*.

"Let's get you inside," Owen said gruffly, clearly as moved as Cal was. His gaze moved to Cal. "And figure out how to stop this."

NORAH HAD TO hold herself back from running into the house. She wanted to hold her baby, except a sharp bark was their first greeting as Hero raced over to them. But, to Norah's surprise, he ran right to Owen.

He jumped and whined, his tail wagging as he pranced in a circle around Owen, whose face broke out into what was clearly an uncharacteristic grin. "There's a buddy," he said, kneeling down and petting the dog, accepting exuberant face licks.

"You know the dog?" Cal asked, coming around the side of the car and immediately sliding his arm around Norah's waist. She leaned into him, grateful for the connection. She knew she had to come to some place of strength, but she was struggling.

"Hero is my dog. I gave him to Norah for protection."

Cal's grip tightened a little bit. "He did a hell of a job," he said gruffly.

But Norah was more than a little taken aback. "Hero. That's his name?"

Owen nodded as he stood.

She looked up at Cal. "That's what I've been calling him. I thought I made it up, but I remembered."

"You're remembering lots of things," he said reassuringly.

But she wasn't remembering the important ones. Her father, the villain. Whoever had attempted to kill her. All the important information was still stubbornly behind some fog.

The front door opened and Jessie stepped out, Evelyn in her arms. Unable to stop herself now, Norah rushed forward. Jessie smiled warmly and easily handed Evelyn over. "She's been very good, but she missed her mama."

Norah held her close and was rewarded with a big smile. She felt as though her heart might break into a million pieces. "Oh, baby. Mama missed you." She held the wriggling baby tight and breathed.

Here was her center. No matter what happened, no matter what was true, the only thing that mattered was keeping her baby safe.

She felt Cal come up behind her and turned to face him, and adjusted Evelyn so she could see him too. "Daddy too," she murmured, then looked up at Cal.

No matter what happened to her, she didn't think she'd ever forget the way Cal's expression changed. Like he felt exactly what she did. Evelyn was their anchor, their center, and the reason they'd keep fighting whatever all *this* was.

People wanted them dead for whatever insane reasons, but they would keep fighting it. For their daughter.

He touched Evelyn's cheek and said nothing, but Norah felt everything he was feeling. He tried to hide it behind that tough, stoic military act, but she saw all the longing and worry and love reflected in his eyes.

"Let's get inside," he said brusquely, his gaze moving away from Evelyn and to the world around them. So many threats and who knew where they were all coming from.

But finally, *finally* she had her husband back. She knew he had reservations about that.

But she didn't. Couldn't.

They all moved inside, and as if some signal had been sent around, everyone came to congregate in the living room. There were attempts at smiles, but most of the expressions were grim—especially from the men when they saw Owen.

They all held the exact same kind of tension in their shoulders—not exactly a bad tension, just a watchful one. Then Dunne and Quinn stepped in from the kitchen, grinning at each other as if they'd just been sharing some joke.

But when Dunne looked into the room and saw his father, the smile on his face slowly faded. His posture notably changed, somehow going straighter. Quinn gave him a puzzled look.

"Dad," Dunne finally said. Quinn's eyes widened.

Owen stood military-straight, as if inspecting his son. And the woman who'd just dropped his hand like it was on fire. "Dunne."

"This is a…surprise," Dunne managed.

"Well, I have some information, and it seemed like we were at the point in this whole mess it made more sense for me to come and sit down with you all and come up with a plan."

Dunne nodded, wordlessly. The he cleared his throat. "Ah, this is…"

"Quinn Peterson. I know." Owen stepped forward and held out his hand.

Quinn studied it like it was a snake that might bite. "Why does he know my name?" she asked Dunne in a low voice.

"I know lots of things," Owen said, smiling genially, which seemed like an odd change from how he usually acted. But maybe Norah just couldn't remember his affable side. "For now, let's focus on what I know about figuring out how to keep the men safe. Where can we all sit comfortably? In here?" Owen walked into the kitchen.

Henry and Jessie followed, Landon and Hazeleigh not far behind. Zara and Kate ducked into the kitchen. Brody gave Dunne's shoulder a slap as he passed, but Dunne and Quinn still just stood there, as if they were frozen.

Quinn was the first to come out of it. She looked at the people still in the room. "Well, keeping the men safe. That's a nice change of events," she said brightly, then turned and strode into the kitchen as if she was marching into battle herself.

Dunne followed her and Cal stepped forward, but Norah stopped him. "Cal..."

He looked down at her. Then melted her heart by touching her cheek, just the way he'd touched Evelyn's. "You're tired."

"I know I should help, and remember, and—"

"You're tired, and still healing. Why don't you go lie down? I'll fill you in on everything, I promise."

Maybe it was the coward's way out, but that was exactly what Norah did. Not just because she was tired, but because she didn't know how to face everyone and still not remember. To face all these people knowing she had the key to this whole thing somewhere locked inside of her—but she couldn't get it out.

She took Evelyn to the room she'd been staying in, curled up with her in the little bed, and tried to relax. Rest.

But her mind whirled, and even when Evelyn dozed off, Norah didn't. She watched her daughter sleep, and desperately tried to remember anything. *Anything.*

She must have finally dozed, because she woke with a start. Evelyn was still fast asleep, but when she looked behind her, Cal stood in the doorway. Watching them.

"How long did I sleep?"

"Probably not long enough," he replied, stepping inside. His gaze traced over her and Evelyn. She patted the mattress so he'd take a seat next to her.

She shifted, being careful not to disturb the bed too much, so she could curl next to Cal, and look at their daughter. *Theirs.*

Finally. Finally. This was everything she'd ever wanted. Right here. And yes, danger existed, but life was never going to be *easy*. They'd lost, they'd fought. Those things left scars.

But the love they shared, their daughter…these were the things scars healed for.

Norah looked up at her husband. She'd thought he was gone. Dead. But here he was. "What do you want, Cal?"

He stiffened and kept his gaze firmly on Evelyn. "You to be safe."

"No, I mean out of your life. What do you *want*?"

He looked up at the ceiling, looking as helpless as

she'd ever seen him. "It doesn't matter. What matters is keeping you safe."

"More than that matters. We matter. You're my husband."

He shook his head. "Callum Young was your husband, Norah. I'm not him anymore." But he didn't meet her gaze, and she saw that for what it was worth.

God, she hoped she saw that for what it was. "Is that what you want?" she asked, meaning to sound demanding, but her voice only came out in a pained whisper.

"It's what *is*."

"I'm not asking what *is*. I'm asking what *you* want. Not what you should want. Not what's best for me or for Evelyn. I want to know what you want."

His jaw tightened, and for the longest time she didn't think he'd look at her. But eventually his gaze moved. Met hers.

"I want you. Both of you. I want my family under this roof. Without danger, without questions. I want the life I promised you, Norah."

"You know that's what I want too."

"You don't remem—"

She moved up, cut off his words by pressing her mouth to his. The only man she'd ever loved. And no matter what she remembered or didn't, she knew that love was the core of everything that mattered. "I love you, Callum," she said against his mouth. "Whether you're Cal Young or Cal Thompson or someone else altogether."

She cupped his face with her hand, and he stared

at her. Because she knew he was fighting his internal wars. And that was okay because she always won them for him. Always. “No matter what happens, you’ll never get rid of us. No matter what I remember or don’t, I’ll always love you. No matter what’s changed, or what will, you are my home, and I’m yours. We have already lost enough. I refuse to lose more.”

He dropped his forehead to hers. “You never would let me go.”

She shook her head. “Never.”

“I love you, Norah.” This time, he pressed his mouth to hers. And for a few moments, her fears and worries evaporated, because she’d thought she’d lost him, in so many ways, but here they were.

He sighed against her mouth, adjusted their position so they could hold on to each other and watch Evelyn sleep. She relaxed against his chest, and into his arms, and was so full of love she thought she might burst.

Until Cal spoke. “You were dreaming when I walked in. Talking in your sleep.”

She snuggled in closer. “Oh yeah? About what?”

“Someone named Tara.”

And all that warmth, and joy, disappeared in an instant and turned bitterly cold in her chest.

Chapter Eighteen

Cal felt the way she stiffened, but she didn't speak. He didn't know whether to push, or to wait. He'd never heard her speak of a Tara before, and she hadn't sounded...distressed in her sleep, so he hadn't really thought it would unlock some terrible memory.

But her breath was coming in short little pants, and she didn't answer him.

"Norah."

"I don't..." She sucked in a deep breath, then looked up at him. All the worry and confusion and *hurt* of the past few days was back on her face, and he was sorry to have put it there. "I don't remember. I don't know a Tara that I can think of, but when you said that name I just feel...cold."

He rubbed his hands up and down her arms, trying to give her some semblance of warmth. "Maybe Owen knows."

She nodded, but she was clearly distracted.

"I'll go ask."

Norah shook her head, and it was like she was shaking herself. "No. I'll ask him." Then she shook her head once more. "I'll see if I can get Evelyn down in her crib, and *we'll* go ask him." She looked up at him, blue eyes big and sad. But she still had hope, and it was that hope that had always snuck under all his defenses. Because he had none, and hers was irresistible.

"I'll put her down," he said, not sure why his voice came out so hoarse. Or why, when he'd handled guns and bombs and dying men, sliding his hands under his child felt like the most dangerous thing he'd ever done.

But Norah was here, and his child was here, and she was right, of course. She'd always been right. When he saw the complications, she held on to all that hope and found solutions.

Whatever happened, whatever came for them, they'd fight it together. Come out on the other side together. They'd already lost enough. He gently maneuvered Evelyn from the bed to her little crib.

She scrunched up her little face, wriggled a little bit, but then slowly settled back into a sound sleep. Norah turned on the baby monitor and attached the receiver to her belt.

For a moment, they stood side by side, watching their daughter sleep.

Cal hadn't cared about more than surviving in a very long time. But now, it was *all* he cared about. He pressed a kiss to Norah's temple and then they walked out into the kitchen where Owen, Landon, Henry, Dunne and Quinn had congregated around the table.

"Owen, do you know a Tara who might connect to all of this?" Norah asked, and he could feel her apprehension, but her voice was controlled and calm.

Owen lifted his gaze to Norah, but his expression was blank. There was no visible reaction to the name—carefully so. Which was reaction enough.

"You do," Cal said flatly. It seemed so unfair Owen knew all these things, and Norah couldn't remember them.

"I know a few," Owen hedged.

"I said the name in my sleep. I have this…awful physical reaction when I hear her name. But I don't know who she is. Owen, who is she?"

Owen scraped a hand over his face. "Tara Angelo was a young woman who worked in your father's office years ago."

"And?"

"I don't know for sure that it was true, but the rumor was they had an…affair."

"How many years ago?" Norah demanded, her hand finding Cal's.

Owen hesitated, but then seemed to realize there was no way out of this conversation. "Ten."

"Ten years ago. *Ten* years ago?"

Owen looked at Norah, then Cal apologetically. "Yes."

"An affair. When my mother died. You… We've been looking into this all this time and you never said…" She put a hand to her temple, anger clearly warring with her pockets of memory loss. "Or did you?"

Owen shook his head. “I didn’t mention it. I didn’t see the point. When I was looking into everything you brought to me, her name came up. Some old office gossip. But there’s no connection there. Maybe it’s a motive for your father’s…potential involvement in your mother’s death, but it doesn’t have anything to do with now. I don’t think this is quite the breakthrough you’re hoping for, Norah. I’m sorry.”

“Then why do *I* have a reaction to the name?” Norah demanded before Cal could demand for her. “Why do *I* seem to know who she is?”

“Tara Angelo. Age thirty-one. Currently living in Philadelphia, working in a dentist’s office as an office manager,” Landon read, clearly having looked her up on his computer. But his eyebrows drew together. “She was reported missing three weeks ago.” Landon looked up at Cal. “Two days before Norah reported her father missing.”

“I’d call that a damn connection,” Cal said, glaring at Owen.

“My father had an affair around the time he may have killed my mother. Now this woman disappears around the same time my father supposedly did?” Norah shook her head, her hands curling into fists. “But it doesn’t make *sense*.”

She sounded so lost, and Cal wished he had any kind of comfort to give her, but none of this made sense, and the more they found, the more confused he felt.

“However odd that may seem, she hasn’t shown

up in any of our surveillance of your father," Owen said. "If this connects, it's not to him."

"That you know of. Clearly you don't know everything or we wouldn't be in this mess."

Norah sighed. "It isn't his fault."

Cal didn't want to agree with her because it felt good to have someone to blame. Someone to lash out at. But he saw an opportunity to point something out. "Then it isn't yours," Cal reminded her, holding her close to his side.

She frowned a little at that, but Cal figured he'd scored a point in favor of her not being so damn hard on herself.

"Let's try none of this is anyone's fault except the people trying to murder," Owen said, and clearly he felt like he was in charge of the situation. He was the superior officer, after all.

But weren't his brothers always telling him they weren't in the military any longer, so there were no leaders, no superiors? Just a team. Just brothers.

Owen was still in the military. Still used to calling the shots. Being the one in charge, and occasionally keeping pertinent details to himself. It had taken Cal a *long* time to get over that, so he thought he understood where Owen was coming from.

"You didn't find a connection between Tara and my father *now*, but what about a connection between Tara and me?"

Owen shook his head. "Not on paper."

All eyes turned to Norah, and Cal wished he could hide her from everyone's intent gaze. She already blamed herself for so much, and for not remembering. The pressure certainly wasn't helping her brain heal.

"I've never had amnesia," Quinn offered. "But I've been terrorized a time or two. You feel that creepy cold feeling when you hear her name? My bet is she has something to do with those bruises on your neck."

Norah brought her fingers up to her collar, but she said nothing.

"Bruises that didn't happen in DC," Cal muttered to himself, trying to tie all the pieces together so Norah didn't feel pressured to remember. "They happened *after* you knew I was alive, knew where I was. When you were on your way here."

Cal considered the possibility Elliot had tried to kill her because she knew Cal was alive, but Elliot hadn't left DC. He could have sent one of his men after her. It was all possible. But the more they looked into this, the more it seemed like two separate events that just were happening on a similar timeline. Did they connect at all?

Quinn choked on the sip of water she'd just taken. She coughed, pointing at Landon's computer screen. "Holy—" she croaked. "That's this Tara woman?" At Landon's nod, she looked up and met Cal's gaze. "I *know* her."

NORAH WAS GRATEFUL for Quinn, and probably not for any of the reasons she should be. But the attention wasn't on her anymore.

Because she didn't remember. No matter how hard she tried, she could not find facts in her foggy memories. She could not manage to find all the information that would stop this.

Information she had, somewhere deep inside her.

"What do you mean you know her?" So many voices demanded Norah couldn't even keep them all straight. She wanted to put her hands over her ears and go back to the little room with Evelyn and block this all out.

But it was her life, her mess, and she was so incredibly lucky she had all these people who wanted to untangle it for her, but that didn't mean she could just...let them. Not when so much was at stake.

Quinn looked over at Dunne. "Remember the pushy contractor I've been telling you about?" She looked at the group at the table. "Jessie and I are trying to make the Peterson ranch house livable, right? We have a contractor, and I've been dealing with him and he's fine enough. Work is about to start. But this lady shows up and starts saying she can do a better job, give me a better deal. Real pushy. I can't stand pushy."

Landon snorted. "Pot. Kettle."

Quinn gave him a dirty look, but she pointed to the screen again. "That's *her.* Her hair is dark now, and she told me her name was Marie, but that's her. I'm like ninety-nine percent sure."

"Marie," Norah said, and it was hard to stay tethered to this moment, with a buzzing kind of panic taking up space in her brain and her knees threatening to give out.

She heard Cal swear next to her, and she knew he wanted to leap into action. But he stayed put and held her upright.

"Can you get in contact with her?" Owen demanded.

Quinn nodded. "She gave me her card, multiple times. I didn't keep it, but I think I just crumpled it up and tossed it in the truck. If I don't have her number, I'm sure she'll show up again."

"I'll go find it," Henry said, moving quickly outside. Then it was a flurry of action. All the men were *talking*, moving. Typing on computers and discussing plans and… Norah knew she should be part of it. She should demand a place at the table.

She wanted to run and hide. Instead, she took a deep breath and disentangled herself from Cal. He was distracted enough to let her, since he was arguing with Owen. Norah went over to where Quinn stood in the corner, biting her thumbnail.

"Hey, I'm sorry—"

"Sorry that you've given us a lead?" Norah replied before Quinn could finish the apology.

Quinn smiled ruefully. "Not much of one."

"More than I had," Norah replied. "If Cal hadn't heard me talking in my sleep, we'd still be in the dark." She looked at the table. They were all so intent on *acting*, when she felt mired in…something else.

They needed more information. They needed her

to remember. She looked over Landon's shoulder at the picture on his screen, but no magical memory of who Tara was to her popped up into her brain. Just a soul-deep need to look away. To *get* away.

But it was that feeling, time and again, that led her to remembering. Not plans. Not moving forward. But information. Pictures. Being reminded of things.

"Quinn, can you tell me… Whatever she said to you the times you spoke? Whatever you remember. Even if it seemed boring."

Quinn nodded. "Yeah. Yeah, look… I'll admit I haven't paid attention too closely. I already hired a contractor for the house. But she just shows up one day, said she's had her eye on the house for a while—I doubt it, it's in the middle of nowhere. Tried to hard sell me and upsell me. But I hired this old guy who tells the worst jokes and has like fifty grandkids he lets work for him. Who's going to fire that guy for some pushy lady? Then she gives me some speech about women sticking together, like *I* haven't been personally victimized by more men than I care to count."

Quinn scowled. "It was just all manipulation, you know? Maybe some folks fall for it, and look, it's a big job. Total money pit. Definitely going to earn anybody a lot of money. I figured it had something to do with all that publicity about Jessie and me getting the gold."

Norah nodded. For a wild minute she just wanted to laugh. She was in the middle of Wyoming, with people who had inherited hidden gold treasure, and had long-lost identical twin sisters, six military men who were living under assumed names, and whatever else strange, bizarre backstories.

Her husband was alive. She had some warped form of amnesia.

Quinn patted her shoulder awkwardly. "Hey, this is a lot. You don't have to hold it all together, you know? You must be tired."

Norah shook her head, even though she probably *was* tired somewhere underneath the wired feeling of being so close to a memory she couldn't seem to get her hands on. "Is that all? That she wanted the job?"

Quinn considered, but the silence stretched out. Whatever interactions she'd had with the woman were through her own lens, so of course there wouldn't be any connection. Besides, the men were looking into her. They'd think of some plan to talk to her. They had a name, confirmation she was here. They'd find her and deal with her, this woman Norah couldn't remember. Who had once had an affair with her father but otherwise didn't connect.

Norah sighed. "Well, thank you. You've given us something to go on." She tried to smile at Quinn.

The baby monitor hooked to her belt loop gave a little blip of static as it did sometimes, and when no cry came through Norah knew it was just Evelyn moving in her sleep.

"Wait a sec," Quinn said, staring at the baby monitor. "One weird thing. She asked if I had kids. Big house, right? She asked if I had a lot of kids to fill it up. I told her no. She asked if I ever babysat. And I was like, no, I'm an adult woman who grew up in a cult, leave me be, lady, you know?"

Norah definitely did not know, but she tried to smile at Quinn.

"But it was like… The question itself wasn't weird, but it was the intensity and the way she wouldn't let it go. Dunne was there with me that day, and she was like he's a handsome guy, don't you want his babies? Kinda flirty, but mostly *weird*."

Babies. Baby. That cold feeling spread, and she kept listening to Quinn talk about the moment, but she stared at the picture on the computer screen. Focused on the woman's face. It was a driver's license picture, so it was small, head-on, but this woman… this woman and babies…

"And I was like, whoa, lady, we are *dating*, and I am a mess who didn't have a mother. I'm hardly ready to *become* one. And I bet Dunne remembers this part, she got all…weird. Like weirder. Wide-eyed and almost like she was in some kind of trance. Right, Dunne?"

Norah was only half listening, staring at the pictures so hard dots started to form in her vision, but Dunne's voice pierced through.

"Yeah, it was definitely off. Quinn and I wrote it off as some ploy. Like Quinn said, do whatever it took to manipulate Quinn into giving her the gold money. It was strange, but we just figured it was that. She said something about being a mother, didn't she?"

"Yeah, I asked if she had kids since she was so obsessed with them," Quinn said.

"And she said *not yet, but soon.*"

"Oh, right. *Right.*" Quinn snapped her fingers and Norah startled. Her head pounded and she felt that untethered feeling again, but Cal was too busy arguing with Owen to be her anchor. The baby monitor crackled again, just static.

The cold trickled down her spine. She remembered something. Something fuzzy and confusing, but terrifying. "She wants Evelyn."

"Wait. What?"

"I don't know. But I…" It was still hazy. The memory. The images jumbled together without much sense. But it was coming back. It had to come back. *She's mine. You don't deserve her. She's going to be mine.* "That's what she wanted. Not me dead. She wanted my baby."

And when the static came through the monitor this time, followed by Hero getting to his feet and letting out a bark, Norah didn't hesitate. She sprinted for the bedroom, knocking over a chair on her way.

Chapter Nineteen

"We are absolutely not using Norah as *bait,*" Cal said to Owen, growing more and more frustrated with Owen's plans that *all* seemed to put Norah in the middle of danger.

"If we're going to create the element of surprise—"

"Screw surprise," Cal muttered. He glanced back at Norah, who stood talking with Quinn and Dunne. She looked too pale. Too…fragile.

He knew she wasn't. Somehow she'd survived all this, gotten here without any help from him or anyone, really. But knowing how strong she could be didn't make it any easier to let her stand on her own two feet. He didn't want her to have to *be* strong.

Cal sighed. He didn't know how to fix this, but he supposed this Tara woman was a step in the right dire—

Norah darted out of the kitchen, knocking over one of the empty chairs as she rushed toward the bedroom. Cal didn't think, he followed, though Dunne and Quinn were on Norah's heels as well.

They all crowded into the room, even though Cal had no idea why. He only knew something was wrong, and he needed to fix it.

But the window was open. The curtains fluttered in the breeze.

And the crib was empty.

Cal felt his entire life end, right there. But then a little cry sounded, and Norah turned around, Evelyn cradled close to her chest. Still, she was pale and shaking. "I didn't leave that window open. I did not." She said it so defiantly. Like they'd try to argue with her when he was just as sure as she was that the window hadn't been left open.

"I'll go outside and check the window," Landon said.

"Henry's out there," Dunne reminded him. "Stick together."

"Hero jumped out," Norah said, her voice creaky. "He just jumped right out that window."

"I'll check on—"

A gunshot echoed through the slowly falling evening. And then another. It was another race of bodies—those behind him turning out of the room, but Cal figured it was just as easy to pretzel himself out the window.

Henry was leaning against the house, holding his side. "I'm good. Thanks to the dog barking, I think. Nicked me, but I'm good," he said. "It was a woman. Holding a bundle. She ran off. She had… She didn't have the baby?"

Cal surveyed the yard. Dusk had fallen, and he saw no sign of whoever had been at the window. "No."

"She made it look like she did. Or I would have shot."

Landon and Brody came around the side of the house. "No sign of anyone out front," they said. Dunne followed, his pace severely slowed by his limp.

"I thought you had cameras?" Cal demanded of Landon.

"I do," Landon said grimly. "Nothing changed on my end. Which means she had to have tampered with them."

"Explains why she was quiet for a few days. Figuring out how to get around the security," Henry said. "We've got to move before she can regroup and get around them again."

Cal nodded. "We'll fan out. Find her."

"The dog ran after her," Henry said.

Cal nodded. "Good. This ends now." He strode back to the open window and poked his head in. Norah stood with Quinn, holding Evelyn tightly to her chest. He handed Norah his gun. "Stay here."

She tried to reach out with her free hand and grab him, but he backed away. "Callum."

"Listen to me. She wants Evelyn, so you need to stay here where it's safe and protect her. We're going after her."

Quinn gave Norah's shoulder a pat and took the

gun Cal still held out. "We'll handle the home front." She gave Norah a tight smile. "That's what women do," she said with a wink.

He knew Norah wasn't happy with the situation, but he couldn't wait for her to be. They needed to stop this. Now.

Norah moved forward and handed the gun back to him. "You take this. There are more in this house, right Quinn?"

Quinn nodded.

"You take the gun. Quinn will get me another one. You protect yourself. Be careful. Be… Please."

Cal took the gun and nodded. "I'll be back," he said. A promise. A vow.

He turned back to the men. He didn't want to leave Norah and Evelyn, but they couldn't keep holding close and tight and hoping for this to be over.

He wasn't leaving her alone. She had all the women, plus Jake, and…

He turned to Owen, who had come around back after Dunne. Cal wasn't 100 percent certain he trusted the man, but he didn't know the ranch like the rest of them did. He looked at Dunne, and they'd been brothers long enough to know…

Dunne shrugged, a clear sign he didn't know whether to trust his father either. Damn.

"All right. Owen, you're with me," Cal said. "Henry and Dunne—"

"I'm not staying back," Henry said grimly. "She shot me. I'm going after her."

Again, Cal turned to Dunne. Dunne gave a short nod, that Henry was okay and would be without immediate medical attention. "We'll take the front," he said. "In case she doubles back."

Cal nodded. "Brody and Landon, you're team three. Owen and I will head west. You'll head east. This ends tonight."

All the men around him nodded, and then set about to follow his orders.

Cal gave one last look at the window. It was now closed, but Norah stood behind the glass, Evelyn snuggled to her chest.

His family. His heart.

Yeah, this was going to end tonight.

NORAH STOOD IN the little bedroom while Quinn went to fetch her a gun. She felt…stupid and helpless. A pointless fixture in all this danger, and it infuriated her. Probably more than it should, because her role in this was just as important, if not the most important.

Take care of her baby.

"I'm so sorry, Ev," she whispered, rubbing her cheek against the baby's temple. "I don't know how we got into this mess." She sighed. She expected Quinn to return quickly, but when she didn't a little trickle of fear began to cause her heartbeat to race again.

"It's okay," she whispered, trying to convince herself she was talking to Evelyn and not herself. "It's going to be okay." She surveyed the room and looked for something that could be a weapon. But before she could find anything, the door squeaked open. Thank goodness, Quinn was back and—Norah stopped and turned around, speechless, at the appearance of a strange woman in the room.

No, not a strange woman. Tara, just like the picture, but with dark hair.

"How…"

Tara rolled her eyes. "Do you know how *predictable* people can be? Military men always want to be tactical. Fan out. Blah, blah, blah. The dog gave me a start, but I was ready for him." She smirked.

Hero. "You hurt my dog?"

Tara shrugged. "Your *dog* almost killed me before. Kept me from finishing my job. He deserved everything he got out in those woods. And while the men were blabbing about *plans*, I could sneak into the stables, scare that little girl and distract everyone here."

Sarabeth.

"She'll be fine. I don't hurt kids." Tara smiled as Evelyn fussed in Norah's arms. "I'm an excellent mother. Or I'm going to be."

Norah felt that same cold from before. When she heard the name *Tara.* She still had no memory of why. The woman stepped forward and held out her arms. "Now, don't be stupid this time. Give me my baby."

This time.

She'd tried before. She'd tried to take Evelyn before. "You know I won't give her up." She would fight tooth and nail. Just like last time. *Last* time. When she'd been on her way to Cal, and gotten a ride from this woman, thinking she was just a harmless ride service driver.

But she'd tried to take Evelyn. Tried to kill Norah with her bare hands. Instead, Hero had attacked and Norah had somehow managed to run. Run toward Cal.

"The dog is gone. Your little heroes are gone. It's so easy to manipulate these military men. Shoot one. Shoot another. Pit them against each other. A little tit for tat. Because no, your hero won't be coming to save you. Let's just say they're all otherwise occupied. For good."

"What?"

The woman moved around the room. "Your father wanted the men? I handed them over. Told him I wouldn't hurt you." She laughed. "So predictable. As long as he got what he wanted, he didn't worry about what happened to anyone else. But now, it's time to get what *I* want." Tara stepped closer, still aiming her gun at Norah's head. "Hand her over."

"Never. She is mine. My daughter."

"No, she's mine. Your father promised me a baby. He *promised*. But he's a liar. So. Now I'll have her. You don't have to worry. I'll take good care of her."

Norah wanted to cry. As much as she'd started to remember about her father being a terrible person, there was still a part of her that remembered the mask. Or the man he'd been before. Whatever it was, it hurt that he'd…he'd hurt so many women.

"I'm sorry my father hurt you," Norah managed to say, keeping her voice calm for Evelyn's sake. "But you can't take that out on me."

"Of course I can. You're an obstacle. I'm taking care of it. Just like I took care of your mother."

Norah's body went weak. "What?" she managed to rasp.

"She was the only thing between us, he said. So, I took care of it. I took care of it and her and we were supposed to be together. Then it was *you*. And his job. He was supposed to be *mine*, but he lied. He lied and he lied and he lied. All to get what he wanted. It's my turn." The woman lifted the gun. "Now, I'll get what I deserve."

Norah curled herself around Evelyn, who was starting to cry. She squeezed her eyes shut, desperate to think. She needed that weapon. She needed to fight. She'd survived this woman once, and she would damn well survive her again.

Which was when she realized she still wore the baby monitor receiver on her belt. It wouldn't stop a gun, but it could do some damage if she wielded it right. And if it was really true, that this woman wouldn't hurt Evelyn…

Well, it was worth a shot. Norah would use her body to shield Evelyn no matter what, and she wouldn't be alone forever. Even if the men were out looking for Tara, even if they got caught by her father—she tried not to think about what her father wanted to do to them—there were still people here who would come to help. Once Sarabeth was settled. Eventually.

"Please don't hurt her," Norah said, keeping her voice shaky and weak as she huddled in the corner, hoping her body shielded her hand trying to unhook the monitor from her belt loop.

"Hurt her? I'm going to be her mother now. And she'll never know the difference. And everything will finally be okay. Your father will lose, and I will win."

The gun cocked.

Norah took a deep, steadying breath. She whispered a little assurance to Evelyn, who was wailing now. Then she whirled, flinging the baby monitor as hard as she could at the gun.

It didn't hit the gun, but it caught Tara by enough surprise it did one better. It slammed into her face. Tara let out a howl of pain as the baby monitor clattered to the ground. Evelyn's increasing cries drowned out the sound.

And Norah darted for the door. She thought she'd made it. Thought she could run—just like she had last time—but a sharp pain in her scalp jerked her back.

"You will pay for that," Tara said, giving Norah's hair another jerk.

She cried out in pain, but she wasn't going down

that easy. Not with her daughter in her arms. But before she could decide what to do, something creaked.

"Stop." It was a cold demand from the now open window. Quinn stood there, aiming a gun right at Tara.

Echoed by Jessie at the door, also pointing a gun at the woman.

Tara stood there, hand still in Norah's hair, her nose bleeding. She seethed. "They won't come to save you! They're all going to die. And then so will you."

"Then we'll have to go save them. Drop Norah. Drop the gun."

"Make me," she spat.

Norah made eye contact with Jessie. She looked so cool and calm, and Norah did everything she could to match that look even as Tara's grip tightened in her hair. As she began pulling her closer by her hair, Norah jerked her chin down toward the wriggling Evelyn.

"Now, give her to her new mommy," Tara said, in a creepy singsong voice.

"Make me," Norah replied, mimicking her. She jerked once, hard, and though the grip in her hair didn't loosen, and the pain in her scalp was excruciating, Norah held Evelyn out and Jessie rushed to take her.

The second Evelyn was out of her arms, Norah rammed into Tara. Jessie ran with Evelyn, and Tara screamed in frustrated anger. But they were so close now that she couldn't move her arm to get the gun pointed at Norah easily. Norah grabbed her wrist, and they grappled.

Norah didn't think about Quinn at the window. She didn't think about Jessie running off with Evelyn.

She only thought about doing some damage.

Chapter Twenty

The dark was an obstacle. Cal hadn't brought a flashlight, though Owen had turned his phone's flashlight feature on.

Owen. Cal surveyed him every so often, trying to determine if this would be his downfall. Trusting the man who'd once sent him to war. A man even his own son wasn't sure he could trust.

At least in war he'd always known who'd had his back.

They still did, Cal reminded himself. He still had five brothers right here who were fighting to protect his daughter, his wife and him. Not because he'd ordered them to, but because that was what family did.

"Why are you really here, Owen?" Cal muttered as they moved through the dark otherwise silently. Cal supposed it wasn't the time to be having the conversation, but there was no sign of anyone out here.

Owen turned off his flashlight. "Up there. Two o'clock. You see that?"

Cal looked to where Owen instructed and did see

a little flash of light. It was still a good ways off, but it was something to move toward. "Why are you here, Owen?"

Owen sighed next to him. He didn't turn on his light and they didn't move forward. "Sometimes, it takes a long time to realize the mistakes you made. And that the things you did thinking you were a good friend, a good man, were really just cowardly, because you didn't want to make waves."

"Elaborate."

Owen laughed, a little bitterly. "You were a great soldier, Cal. I could probably use you again, if you wanted, but I doubt you do."

"No, I don't." And it was a strange thing to realize. Because being a soldier had been…everything to him once. Until Norah. Maybe even until Evelyn.

"I had no idea Elliot planned to kill his wife, if that's what happened. I'd heard rumors about the affair way back when. And I'd noticed a change in his demeanor. But I figured those were his issues. His problems. Family, not work. So, I ignored it. And when the pattern started again recently, I would have gone right on ignoring it, but Norah came to me. With all these fears and what should have been crazy accusations, but they weren't. I couldn't even muster up surprise. I should have been horrified. But it just felt…grim."

Cal didn't know what to say to that.

"I'm here because I should have said something

then. Before things got so out of hand my own son was somehow in the crosshairs of it all."

"I'm not sure any of that was your responsibility."

"Then whose was it?"

That was the eternal question, wasn't it? How involved to get. How much to stand up and say your piece. When to lie to keep the peace. Still, at some point, you couldn't hold yourself responsible for other people's issues. "Elliot's mostly."

Owen sighed again. "Then once we stop this Tara woman, let's stop him."

They moved toward the light. A team, and sure Owen could have been lying still, but it didn't add up. And though Cal knew Owen and Dunne had a complicated relationship, it wasn't *bad.*

So, he took a leap of faith—because it was what Norah would have done. She'd put her trust in Owen before, and now Cal had to do the same.

They walked, focusing on the light, and Cal didn't doubt Brody and Landon would be doing the same on the east side of the property. It was quite possible that whoever had tried to take Evelyn—whether it was Tara or someone else—hadn't acted alone. They'd only ever seen evidence of one person lurking around the ranch.

The problem was that even with Landon's cameras and all their perimeter checks and work on the ranch, the land was vast, and the property adjacent to the ranch was just as vast and isolated. It was so easy to hide.

Then Cal heard it, just the tiniest *snick* of something in the dark. Just a shade too loud to be animal. Just a shade too close to ignore. "Behind," Cal called.

He couldn't see in the dark, not really more than shadows, but he had his instincts and his hearing and the training of years and years of combat. He punched out—and hit somebody. Not Owen.

He heard a thud, and Owen's quiet swear. So, there were at least two assailants. There was nothing else to do but fight. It was too dark to shoot when Owen was by his side, also fighting someone, so Cal punched, kicked, elbowed and used his gun as a weapon of blunt force trauma rather than to shoot.

He heard another person—so at least three. One of the ones fighting Cal managed to kick him so hard he lost his grip on the gun. Still, Cal kicked out, rolled and managed to get the attacker on the ground. He just needed to wrestle the gun from him and—

A gunshot pierced through the quiet night around them, and Cal was grateful he didn't feel the familiar pain of bullet ripping through flesh, but he didn't know who had shot or potentially been shot.

And then a voice rang out, loud and commanding as a flashlight popped on. "That'll be enough." It was Elliot's voice. A military command that had the third man backing off, and the two injured men crawling over to where he stood. "You've always been an excellent fighter, Cal. Too bad you're such a lying piece of scum too. But I knew I'd need more than just these three." He looked at his men with disgust. Then at the man with Cal.

"Owen." Elliot seemed genuinely surprised. "You… This doesn't involve you."

"You want my son dead. I think it does."

"It isn't personal."

"Oh, well, then. Please kill my only child," Owen returned caustically. "What happened to you?"

Elliot straightened, his chest puffing out. "Nothing happened to me. I'm making things right. Making sure that everyone who lied to me pays."

"What about the people you lied to?"

"I'm not a liar. I do what's right."

"You had your wife killed."

"I did no such thing. That stupid woman misconstrued everything I said. She did everything wrong and made a mess. That's her fault and her problem, not mine."

That stupid woman... "You mean Tara?" Cal asked, desperate to connect the dots.

Elliot scoffed. "Tara." He shook his head. "I don't have anything to do with that nutcase anymore. She was a means to an end."

"An end that tried to steal my child from her mother," Cal returned, trying to keep his fury contained enough that he didn't make a grave mistake. "It's one thing to want to kill me, but you want your own granddaughter—"

"Your bastard. Your *lie. Not* my granddaughter," Elliot said, with such venom Cal couldn't even find words. Who could be so vile when talking about their own flesh and blood? A *baby.* "I don't care about that abomination. Tara can do whatever she wants with her. I want *you*, and your brothers. You tried to make a fool out of me. Well, we'll see who gets the last laugh."

A light clicked on, bright and directly in Cal's eyes. He squinted against it, determined not to close his eyes completely even as it blinded him.

The illuminated space was a hole that clearly had been recently dug. Deep and wide enough to bury a few people, as Cal figured that was the point. Because down inside the hole were explosives.

"Once your *brothers* arrive, they'll join you here. And they'll arrive. All of them, to save their leader. So honorable, so upstanding. Defiling my daughter and forcing her to lie to me."

"You're delusional if you think that's what happened."

"I know it's what happened. My daughter would never lie to me, leave me, betray me. You made her. *You.*"

"You had her mother killed. You told her I was dead. You told me she was dead. You're the liar. The one who betrayed—"

Elliot raised a gun, pointed it at Cal's head. "I was going to blow you all up, but this is fine. I'll shoot you and save the explosives for your bothers. No one lies to me. No one."

Before Cal could jump out of the way or grab one

of the guns from the men behind him, an odd growl sounded in the dark, followed by a bark and a flurry of movement.

Elliot went down, even as a gunshot went off. Cal heard it buzz by him, freezing him for a second before he realized how close it had been to his head and threw himself onto the ground. Owen ran forward and Landon and Brody appeared as Cal got back to his feet. Brody and Landon helped Owen detain the men who'd been fighting them, getting rid of their guns and tying them up. Cal went over to Hero, picked up the gun the dog had wrestled out of Elliot's grasp.

Elliot thrashed, his arm bloody and Hero standing on his chest, snarling menacingly. Red and blue lights flashed in the distance. Cops.

Never in his life had he been so *glad* to see law enforcement, and as much as identities were at stake, Elliot needed to be arrested and tried for *all* his crimes.

Hero growled at the approaching officers, but Cal petted his head. "It's all right, boy. It's all right. You really are a hero."

Hero had blood on him, and Cal realized he'd been injured. Elliot or one of his men had shot him. "Jesus. We need a vet." He pulled the dog off Elliot as law enforcement came with guns and handcuffs and backup.

Backup. Help.

One of the cops came over, and then spoke into

his walkie-talkie, asking for a veterinarian. "Looks shallow, but we'll get him taken care of."

Cal nodded, then pressed his face into the dog's fur for one second, trying to collect himself. "You deserve a medal, champ." He looked up at the cop. "The house? The woman who tried to take the baby?"

"We've got officers at the house as well." But he didn't give any more information as the team of officers began dragging men to their truck.

"Text from Jake," Landon said, jogging over and out of breath. "They've got Tara. Zara called Thomas the minute gunshots started back at the house," he said, referring to Zara's cousin who was a police officer with the county. "Once the cops got to the house and found out what was going on, they sent a team out here. So, it's okay. Everyone's okay."

Okay. Cal didn't know how to believe it until he held his family in his arms.

NORAH WAS STILL SHAKING. Her arms burned where Tara had scratched her, and her eye was swelling where the woman had managed to elbow her.

But Tara had fared much worse. Norah wasn't exactly proud of it—okay, maybe she was. She'd taken care of herself. She'd protected her daughter. And now Tara was in police custody and *they* could deal with the woman who'd wanted to steal her child. The woman who'd conspired to kill her mother.

Norah held Evelyn close to her chest as the kind police officer finished questioning her. He was soft and gentle and paused anytime Evelyn fussed so Norah could calm her. But no matter how calm everyone was, Norah couldn't relax. Not until—

Cal burst through the doors. He'd been through a fight too, she could tell. But he was whole. And alive. That was all that mattered. Before she could even stand, he was at her side, pulling her and Evelyn close.

"You're all right," they said in unison, holding each other so tightly Evelyn began to squirm in protest. They both loosened their hold and looked at each other.

His face was bruised, and his lip and nose were bleeding. But he was okay. He was okay and…

Cal's hands framed her face—his were bruised and bloodied too. "Who did you fight? My father?"

"His men," Cal replied. He touched the edge of her swollen eye in a featherlight caress. "You fought too."

"She gave her hell," Jake offered. "They had to transport Tara to the hospital in police custody."

Norah thought she maybe should feel bad about that. But she didn't. Because they had certainly been through enough hell at the hands of other people. Maybe she could feel some sympathy for Tara, who'd clearly been used by her father, and hadn't been mentally stable to begin with, but that didn't mean she'd ever feel bad for protecting herself and her daughter with her own hands.

"My…father?" she asked tentatively, not sure what

outcome she was hoping for. The man had betrayed her. So many times over. Maybe he hadn't been directly behind her mother's death, but he certainly hadn't handled the situation correctly.

"Hero saved the day again," Owen said—he'd clearly fought too, as he had a bloody lip and torn clothes and was leaning more on one foot than another. "Elliot was about to shoot Cal when Hero jumped in. Your father's injured, but he'll survive."

Norah couldn't take her hands off Evelyn, but she looked at Cal. "I'm sorry. I wish—"

"It's all over now. No apologies on our end necessary. They tried to hurt us. They failed. Now they're going to have every legal repercussion possible stop them from ever hurting us again."

He said it so fiercely, and with such confidence, she thought maybe she really could relax. They'd handled all the threats, and now they were someone else's problem.

"My deputies collected him and his men. They'll need to be checked out by a medic as well, but they're in custody and will stay that way," the police officer said. "We'll call in a federal agency to handle everything and the information Mr. Wilks gave us," he said, nodding at Owen. "I'm sure they'll want to talk to you all, ask a lot of the same questions I already have, but for the time being you can clean up and get some rest. We just ask that you stay put." He offered them a kind smile. "You're safe now."

Safe. *Safe*. Norah leaned into Cal, and for the first

time that day let herself cry. In relief. Even if there were some things she never remembered, they were safe.

They were home.

"I love you," she whispered, as Cal held her tight.

"I love you too," he murmured.

And even in all this pain, she knew that it was going to be okay. Because they finally had each other again. And they had this found family who'd helped protect and save them.

So, no matter what happened in the future, they'd always have this. They'd always have love.

Epilogue

The puppy wouldn't stop barking.

Cal stared at him balefully. "You need some lessons, buddy."

The dog kept yipping, the pink bow around its neck hanging loose because the animal had spent ten minutes this morning trying to tear it off before giving up.

Cal was still waiting for the signal out here on the back porch. It was a beautiful day to celebrate his daughter's first birthday. At home. With his family. All things that even all these months later filled him with a gratitude so big it threatened to take him out at the knees.

But Cal Thompson was stronger than that.

Sarabeth clattered into the kitchen, then flung the screen door open. "It's time," she said, practically jumping with excitement.

Cal grinned at her. She'd always been a resilient thing, but she'd come a long way. She was going to school, caring for the animals on the ranch, so thrilled about becoming a big sister in a few months.

Cal followed Sarabeth into the living room that was decorated to the nines with pink and purple balloons, streamers and all manner of first-birthday decorations. Evelyn stood holding on to Norah's knees, and they both turned and grinned at him when he entered.

"Dog! Dog!" Evelyn babbled, because *dog* was her favorite word and favorite thing in the world. She toddled over to him as he knelt to the ground and held out the dog. Evelyn squealed in delight when the dog started licking her face.

Cal met Norah's gaze over delighted one-year-old and ecstatic puppy. Her eyes were shiny, with happy tears, he knew, their own version of delighted and ecstatic.

Eventually Evelyn opened the rest of her presents, while they all piled around the kitchen table and sang "Happy Birthday." New babies and wives and fiancées and his five brothers. Who had proven to him time and again that they'd never let him be that scared, lonely teenager again.

It was not what Cal could have ever imagined when they'd first stepped foot onto the ranch. That had been survival.

This was life. For all of them. Ever-growing families, hope for the future, and most of all love.

He looked over at Norah, who was trying to hold the squirming puppy still for a picture. She was grinning while Sarabeth talked a mile a minute, trying to get Hero in the frame so he didn't feel left out.

Everyone was shouting suggestions for how to get the picture while Jessie tried to line it up.

Cal just watched, just enjoyed, twisting the wedding ring on his finger. A constant reminder that he'd somehow put one foot in front of the other, just like his mother had told him to do all those years ago.

And her namesake was right here, squealing in glee. His. Growing like a weed, just like all babies should.

Dunne bumped his shoulder to Cal's. "You did all right, Cal."

Cal smiled as Norah grinned over at him when she finally got the picture.

"*We* did great, brother."

Because the Thompson brothers were who they were now, and this was their life. Their family. Their future. Bonded together with love and sacrifice. And the hope Norah had somehow taught him.

Because it turned out, hope was the greatest weapon of all.

* * * * *

COMING NEXT MONTH FROM

HARLEQUIN

INTRIGUE

#2169 MARKED FOR REVENGE

Silver Creek Lawmen: Second Generation • by Delores Fossen

Five months pregnant, Deputy Ava Lawson faces her most unsettling murder case yet—the victims are all found wearing a mask of *her* face. Her ex, Texas Ranger Harley Ryland, will risk everything to protect Ava from the killer out for revenge.

#2170 TEXAS SCANDAL

The Cowboys of Cider Creek • by Barb Han

Socialite Melody Cantor didn't murder the half brother she never knew—and former rodeo star Tiernan Hayes is hell-bent on proving it. But when their investigation exposes dangerous family secrets, will Melody be proven innocent...or collateral damage?

#2171 PURSUIT AT PANTHER POINT

Eagle Mountain: Critical Response • by Cindi Myers

Years ago, tragedy brought sheriff's deputy Lucas Malone and shop owner Anna Trent together. When a missing person case reunites them, they'll battle an unknown drug smuggler—and their developing romantic feelings—to uncover the deadly truth.

#2172 WYOMING MOUNTAIN COLD CASE

Cowboy State Lawmen • by Juno Rushdan

Sheriff Daniel Clark and chief of police Willa Nelson must work together to find a murderer. But when Willa suspects her brother, a former cult member, could be involved, her secrets threaten not only their investigation, but the tender bond the two cops have formed.

#2173 SPECIAL AGENT WITNESS

The Lynleys of Law Enforcement • by R. Barri Flowers

When Homeland Security agent Rosamund Santiago witnesses her partner's execution, federal witness protection is her only hope. Falling for small-town detective Russell Lynley only complicates things. And with a criminal kingpin determined to silence the prosecution's only witness, danger isn't far behind...

#2174 RESOLUTE INVESTIGATION

The Protectors of Boone County, Texas • by Leslie Marshman

Struggling single mom Rachel Miller may have wanted to throttle her deadbeat ex-husband, but kill him? Never. Chief Deputy Adam Reed vows to prove her innocence. But his investigation shifts into bodyguard detail when Rachel becomes the killer's next target.

Get 3 FREE REWARDS!
We'll send you 2 FREE Books plus a FREE Mystery Gift.
CONARD COUNTY: K-9 DETECTIVES
RACHEL LEE
INTRIGUE
ONE NIGHT STANDOFF
NICOLE HELM
FREE
Value Over
$20
HOTSHOT HERO IN DISGUISE
CAVANAUGH JUSTICE: DETECTING A KILLER
Both the Harlequin Intrigue® and Harlequin® Romantic Suspense series feature compelling novels filled with heart-racing action-packed romance that will keep you on the edge of your seat.
YES! Please send me 2 FREE novels from the Harlequin Intrigue or Harlequin Romantic Suspense series and my FREE gift (gift is worth about $10 retail). After receiving them, if I don't wish to receive any more books, I can return the shipping statement marked "cancel." If I don't cancel, I will receive 6 brand-new Harlequin Intrigue Larger-Print books every month and be billed just $6.49 each in the U.S. or $6.99 each in Canada, a savings of at least 13% off the cover price, or 4 brand-new Harlequin Romantic Suspense books every month and be billed just $5.49 each in the U.S. or $6.24 each in Canada, a savings of at least 12% off the cover price. It's quite a bargain! Shipping and handling is just 50¢ per book in the U.S. and $1.25 per book in Canada.* I understand that accepting the 2 free books and gift places me under no obligation to buy anything. I can always return a shipment and cancel at any time by calling the number below. The free books and gift are mine to keep no matter what I decide.
Choose one: ☐ Harlequin Intrigue Larger-Print (199/399 BPA GRMX)
☐ Harlequin Romantic Suspense (240/340 BPA GRMX)
☐ Or Try Both! (199/399 & 240/340 BPA GRQD)
Name (please print)
Address
Apt. #
City
State/Province
Zip/Postal Code
Email: Please check this box ☐ if you would like to receive newsletters and promotional emails from Harlequin Enterprises ULC and its affiliates. You can unsubscribe anytime.
Mail to the Harlequin Reader Service:
IN U.S.A.: P.O. Box 1341, Buffalo, NY 14240-8531
IN CANADA: P.O. Box 603, Fort Erie, Ontario L2A 5X3
Want to try 2 free books from another series? Call 1-800-873-8635 or visit www.ReaderService.com.
*Terms and prices subject to change without notice. Prices do not include sales taxes, which will be charged (if applicable) based on your state or country of residence. Canadian residents will be charged applicable taxes. Offer not valid in Quebec. This offer is limited to one order per household. Books received may not be as shown. Not valid for current subscribers to the Harlequin Intrigue or Harlequin Romantic Suspense series. All orders subject to approval. Credit or debit balances in a customer's account(s) may be offset by any other outstanding balance owed by or to the customer. Please allow 4 to 6 weeks for delivery. Offer available while quantities last.
Your Privacy—Your information is being collected by Harlequin Enterprises ULC, operating as Harlequin Reader Service. For a complete summary of the information we collect, how we use this information and to whom it is disclosed, please visit our privacy notice located at corporate.harlequin.com/privacy-notice. From time to time we may also exchange your personal information with reputable third parties. If you wish to opt out of this sharing of your personal information, please visit readerservice.com/consumerschoice or call 1-800-873-8635. Notice to California Residents—Under California law, you have specific rights to control and access your data. For more information on these rights and how to exercise them, visit corporate.harlequin.com/california-privacy.
HIHRS23